THE
DIVINE
FEMININE

THE
DIVINE FEMININE

EXPLORING THE FEMININE
FACE OF GOD THROUGHOUT
THE WORLD

ANDREW HARVEY
& ANNE BARING

CONARI PRESS

Berkeley, CA

Copyright © 1996 Godsfield Press

Text compilation © 1996 Andrew Harvey and Anne Baring

Originally published by Godsfield Press 1996

DESIGNED AND CREATED BY
THE BRIDGEWATER BOOK COMPANY LTD

The author and publishers are grateful to
the following for the use of pictures:
Bridgeman Art Library; British Museum; Christies, London; Derby Museum;
e.t. archive; Giraudon/Bridgeman Art Library;
Musée d'Aquitaine, Bordeaux; The National Gallery, London

For information, contact:
Conari Press,
2550 Ninth St., Suite 101,
Berkeley, CA 94710

Printed and bound in Hong Kong

Conari Press books are distributed by Publishers Group West.
Library of Congress Cataloging-in-Publication Data

The divine feminine: exploring the feminine face of God throughout the world/
[compiled] by Andrew Harvey and Anne Baring
    p. cm.
Includes bibliographical references and index.
ISBN 1-57324-035-4 (hardcover)
    1. Goddesses. 2. Women and religion. 3. Goddess religion.
    I. Harvey, Andrew, 1952–   II. Baring, Anne, 1931–
BL325.F4D58   1996
291.2'144—dc20   96-3875

Cover: BLUE PROFILE *Odilon Redon* 1840–1916
Half-title: GODDESS OF LAUSSEL c.22,000–18,000 B.C.
Frontispiece: THE BIRTH OF VENUS *Sandro Botticelli* 1445–1510
Page 87: VIRGIN OF THE LILIES *Carlos Schwabe* 1866–1926

CONTENTS

INTRODUCTION

The Eternal Feminine is our guide.

GOETHE

*T*his book is a celebration of the sacred feminine, the feminine face of God as it has been expressed in different cultures all over the world. The Divine Feminine is initiating a crucial new phase in our evolution: urging us to discover a new ethic of responsibility toward the planet; bringing us a new vision of the sacredness and unity of life. Wisdom, justice, beauty, harmony, and compassion are the qualities that have traditionally been identified with the Divine Feminine, yet it is also the irresistible power that destroys old forms and brings new ones into being, the inspiration of the love-in-action that is so needed to transform a culture radically out of touch with its soul. The Divine Feminine is this unseen dimension of soul to which we are connected through our instincts, our feelings, and the longing imagination of our heart. Soul is not limited to our own psychic life. Soul is *invisible* nature, the immense web of relationships that is concealed beneath the veil of matter. It is something both inconceivable and immeasurable to which we belong, in which we live – an intermediate dimension between our physical world and the deep unknowable ground of being.

For many hundreds of years, in the fascination with the development of mind and the technological skills that have given us the power to control nature, the emphasis of Western civilization has been overwhelmingly focused on power, control, and conquest rather than relationship. Now, to balance this one-sided emphasis, the image of the Divine Feminine, together with the mythological tradition that belongs to it, is returning to consciousness. It is reconnecting us to the dimension of the instinctual soul that has been shut away, like the Sleeping Beauty, behind a hedge of thorns. The power and numinosity of the Divine Feminine are needed to arouse the will and energy to act on behalf of life and to restore wholeness and balance to our image of God and so to ourselves. It is awakening us to a new ethic of responsibility, focused beyond tribal and national concerns toward the needs of the planet.

The Divine Mother is asking us to trust and protect life, to work with her in all we do, opening our understanding to the knowledge that we are not separate from herself but an expression of her being. The unknown dimension of soul is our conduit to the Divine. Cut off from soul, the mind becomes impoverished, rigid, dogmatic, and inflated. In compensation for this loss of relationship with instinct, with soul, it becomes driven by the need for ever more power and control. The journey in search of the unknown dimension of soul, back the way we have come, toward nature and the ground of our own nature, is difficult and even dangerous because it asks that we relinquish the certainty of deeply held beliefs, both religious and scientific. It means opening ourselves to discovery.

The Grail of the Feminine is urging us to open our minds to a new vision of reality, a revelation of all cosmic life as a divine unity. For those awakened to this vision, to be born a human being is not to be born into a fallen, flawed world of sin and illusion, cut off from the divine; it is to be born into a world lit by an invisible radiance, ensouled by Divine Presence, graced and sustained by incandescent light and love. Our book is a celebration of this vision.

ANNE BARING and ANDREW HARVEY

CHAPTER ONE

THE GREAT MOTHER

*H*uman consciousness has developed infinitely slowly out of nature. Before we
knew ourselves as human, we were animal and plant, stone and water. For
countless millennia, the potential for human consciousness was hidden within nature,
like a seed buried in the earth. Then, very slowly, it began to differentiate itself from
nature. Deep in our memory is the whole experience of life on this planet: life that
has evolved over the four and a half billion years since its formation; life as hydrogen,
oxygen, and carbon; life as the minutest particles of matter; life as water, fire, air, and
earth; life as rock, soil, plant, insect, bird, animal; life as woman and man evolved from
this eonic experience. Finally the point was reached where life evolved a brain that
enabled us to speak, to formulate thoughts, to communicate with each other through
language, to endow sounds with meaning, and invent writing as a way of transmitting
thoughts. Over these billions of years life on this planet has evolved from
undifferentiated awareness to the self-awareness of our species. All this can be
described as an instinctive process, each phase blending imperceptibly into the next.

As consciousness evolved, the sacred image was like an umbilical cord connecting
us to the deep ground of life. Looking back over the past at the evolution of human
consciousness, it seems to fall into three main stages. During the first stage, broadly

VIRGIN WITH CLOAK OUTSPREAD
15th century

defined as the Paleolithic and Neolithic eras, humanity lived instinctively as the child of the Great Mother, in magical harmony with her body – creation – and knew life and death as two modes of her divine reality. Then this primordial experience began to fade as we gradually developed the capacity for self-awareness and reflective thought and, with this, the power to develop technology and control the environment. During this second phase, human consciousness becomes differentiated from the matrix of nature, and nature is imagined as a great dragon – something to be struggled against, overcome, and controlled.

During this phase of separation, there is a shift of focus from the goddess to the god and a radical split between spirit and nature, dividing the oneness of life into a duality. The god gradually becomes identified with spirit, light, creative mind, and good; and the goddess with nature, matter, darkness, chaos, and evil. Men and women were part of this process of differentiation. Men (unconsciously) aligned themselves with the creator god and the principle of light. Women were associated with nature because of their closeness to instinctual processes. Mythology and religious teaching began to portray the opposition between light and darkness, good and evil, spirit and nature, mind and body. For nearly three thousand years in the three patriarchal religions that evolved from the Middle East, there has been no image of union and relationship between goddess and god, no feminine dimension to the godhead to lend balance and wholeness to our concept of it. This loss of the Divine Feminine has endangered civilization and is clearly reflected in the emphasis on conquest and the drive for power over nature that has created the ethos of modern culture.

Yet, this division of life into two aspects is rooted in the dissociation in ourselves between the conscious, rational mind and the deep, instinctual matrix of soul. It is because of this dissociation, so difficult to understand until the present century, that we have come to divide life into two aspects: spirit and nature, mind and matter. We are now discovering that this is an arbitrary division based on the evolutionary experience of the separation from nature, which has been a painful but necessary phase of our evolution. We need to recover our lost relationship with nature and with soul, and this may be one reason why the image of the Divine Feminine is returning now, during the third phase in the evolution of human consciousness.

Why is the image of the Divine Mother so important? To answer this question, we need look no further than our experience of birth into the world. First of all, there is the experience of the embryo in the womb; the experience of union or fusion and containment within a watery, nurturing matrix. After the traumatic experience of birth and the sudden and violent expulsion from this matrix, the prolongation of the earlier feelings of close relationship, trust, and safety is absolutely vital. Without the consistent and loving care of the mother in early childhood, the child has no trust in itself, no power to survive negative life experiences, no model from which to learn how to nurture and support itself or to care for its children in turn. Its primary response to life is anxiety and fear. It is like a tree with no roots, easily torn up by a storm. Its instincts have been traumatized and damaged. With the love of the mother and trust in her presence, the child grows in strength and confidence and delights in itself and in life. Its primary response is trust.

Without this experience, life becomes threatening, terrifying. Without it, the effort of living exhausts and dispirits. Intense and constant anxiety means that there is no resting place, no solace for loneliness, no feeling that life is something to be trusted and enjoyed. Without this positive image of the feminine, fear, like a deadly parasite, invades the soul and weakens the body. Those cultures that have no image of the Mother in the godhead are vulnerable to immensely powerful unconscious feelings of fear and anxiety, particularly when the emphasis of their religious teaching is on sin and guilt. The compensation for this fear is an insatiable need for power and control over life. How hungry the human heart is for an image of a Divine Mother that would, like an umbilical cord, reconnect it to the Womb of Being, restoring the lost sense of trust and containment in a dimension that may be beyond the reach of our intellect, yet is accessible to us through our deepest instincts.

Those who for centuries have been the transmitters of the patriarchal traditions may not appreciate how deep this need and this longing are; as acutely felt by men as by women. In endowing the transcendent and remote Father with attributes traditionally associated with the Mother, they have to some extent acknowledged this human need. But just as it is the presence of the mother that comforts and reassures the child, so it is the image of the Divine Mother that heals and consoles, sustains and encourages; the image awakens in us the feeling of trust and containment because it reflects our personal experience of our containment in the womb and our earliest human relationship.

This is why the image of the Divine Feminine is returning to us now, to help us recover not only our sense of trust in life but also the relationship with a dimension of consciousness that we have, in our longing to be in control of life, ignored. We ourselves are amazed by the treasure we have brought together in this book and hope that it may open people's awareness to the beauty and power of the texts gathered from all over the world. A knowledge of the symbols the soul uses in dreams to communicate its guidance and its wisdom is essential to an understanding of ourselves, and the greater dimension in which we live. The next chapter explores some of these symbols.

MOTHER AND CHILD *Robin Baring*

CHAPTER TWO

SYMBOLS OF THE DIVINE FEMININE

The oldest and most enduring image of the Divine Feminine made by human hands is the goddess as Great Mother. Humanity has imagined her as the immensity of cosmic space, as the moon, as the earth and nature. She is the age-old symbol of the invisible dimension of soul and the instinctive intelligence that informs it. We live within her being, yet we know almost nothing about her. She is everything that is still unfathomed by us about the nature of the universe, matter, and the invisible energy that circulates through all the different aspects of her being. She spins and weaves the shimmering robe of life in which we live and through which we are connected to all cosmic life.

In all early cultures there are many images that were felt to belong to or describe the Great Mother. Certain forms such as the circle, the oval, the wavy line, the meander, and the spiral are, as early as the Paleolithic era, recognizable as the "signature" of the Feminine. These are found traced on the walls of the caves, on stones and dolmens, and later, in the Neolithic era, on the rounded or egg-shaped pottery vessels, which themselves symbolized the body of the Great Mother. The stone, as the densest, oldest, and most enduring aspect of life on earth, was always an

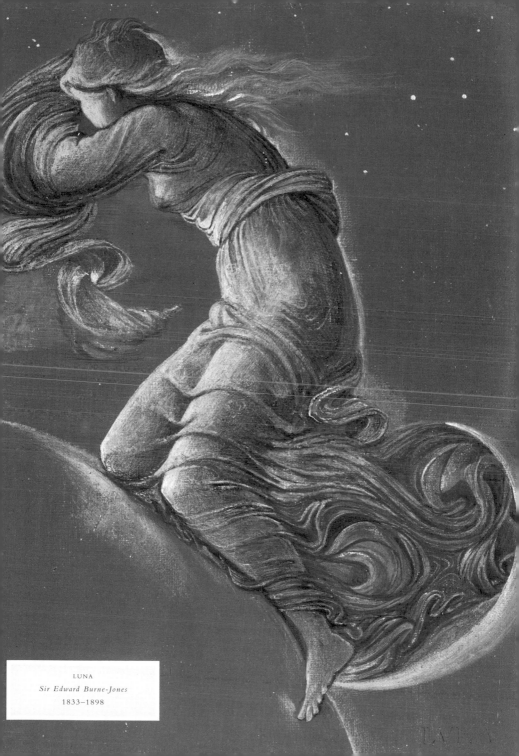

LUNA
Sir Edward Burne-Jones
1833–1898

image of her, a symbol of eternal life. The circle and the egglike oval described her womb and her vulva; the wavy lines were the rainwater or water falling from her breasts, the clouds; the serpent-like spiral, the meander, and the labyrinth were the hidden patterns and pathways of the life force or energy flowing through and connecting the different dimensions of her being.

The moon is perhaps the most ancient symbol of the Feminine. The association between the changing phases of the moon, the seasons of the year, and the life cycle of woman as virgin, mother, and crone is the foundation of an immense mythology inspired by the experience of the moon as an image

THE PREGNANT GODDESS
(FRONT) c. 5000 B.C.

of the unfathomable mystery of life.

It is from the Neolithic era that we have inherited all the images related to the Divine Feminine as an invisible flow of energy that brings life into being, sustains and transforms it, and withdraws it into a hidden dimension for rebirth or regeneration. This process is rhythmic, and rhythm is a primary characteristic of the Feminine, reflected in the ideogram of the wavy line. The movement of the moon, sun and stars, the earth, and water reflect the underlying rhythm of life. All have specific rhythms that affect the rhythm of our own lives.

The sea, along with the moon, is the most ancient image of the Great Mother and the dimension of invisible soul. The great ocean of space is the Great Mother from which everything that we are has emerged. In the Bronze Age mythology of Sumer and India, the Great Mother was the cosmic ocean, and she was personified by a great serpent or dragon. Kuan Yin in the Far East, like the Virgin Mary in the West, is goddess of the sea and protects all who sail on her. The association of sea, water, goddess, and the underlying ground of being is very ancient. Aphrodite was born from the sea foam. Isis and Mary were called "Star of the Sea."

Water most closely resembles the invisible fluid or energy in which all life comes into being. Just as the embryo is suspended in the amniotic fluid of the womb, so we are suspended in the invisible matrix of life. Because our bodies are constituted primarily of water, and because we have all come into being in the watery enclosure of the womb or, at a certain stage of our evolution, we once emerged from water, it holds a numinous fascination for us. In mythology, the longed-for treasure is often to be found across or beneath the sea, or is imagined as the Water of Life. In dreams, immersion in water is, symbolically, to enter into the dimension of the Feminine, the dimension of the instinctual soul to be renewed, cleansed, restored.

Another most important image of the Feminine is the forest. The forest in fairy tales is a metaphor of the soul, through which the hero journeys on a quest. It is the place of trial and danger, of mystery and revelation, where one may be tested by an encounter with an old crone and guided by the strange nonrational wisdom of a helpful animal. In Indian mythology, the forest is Brindavan, the primeval paradise where one may meet with the goddesses and gods.

Animals, birds, and serpents in the Neolithic era were epiphanies of the Great Mother, aspects of her power. Three animals in particular – the lion, the cow, and the snake – always denoted her presence and her power. The goddesses Hathor and Isis in Egypt, and Ninhursag and Inanna in Sumer, were called "The Great Cow," and their temples in Sumer were adorned with enormous horns. Ishtar in Babylon and Durga in India were shown standing on a lion. The many birds that were sacred to the goddess in Neolithic cultures find their way into later mythologies and fairy tales that tell of the magical guidance of swans or doves and other birds. But the butterfly and the bee also belonged to the mythology

THE PREGNANT GODDESS (BACK)
c. 5000 B.C.

of the Great Mother, for she was the queen bee who presided over the hive. There was also a host of smaller animals such as the pig, the doe, even the humble hedgehog. Many of these animals became sacred to her because of their fertility or because, like the bear, their maternal care for their young seemed to reflect the role of the Great Mother.

The snake falls into a separate category, for it has so many associations and meanings and plays so important a role in mythology and dreams that it would need volumes to explore its significance. The snake lives in the desert, in the jungle, in the swamp, under stones, and in secret hidden places. It moves with lightning swiftness yet with an undulating movement. It can suffocate, poison, and devour, yet it is an age-old symbol of healing. It is an image of archaic fear, yet at the same time a symbol of creative spirit and of life's power to renew itself; it is perhaps the oldest known image of the wisdom of instinct. The serpent or snake, like the dragon, is the traditional guardian of the treasure. In the civilizations of Egypt and Mesopotamia, it was the symbol of wisdom until, with the rise of the patriarchal religions, it came to symbolize deception and evil.

Another group of images has evolved from the symbolism of the body of the Great Mother as the container and transformer of life. For Stone Age people, the cave was the Great Mother's womb, the place of mystery where the tribe held its most sacred rites. The symbolism of the womb is reflected in the vessel as the carrier of water and food; in the oven or cooking pot where food is transformed; in the pool, bath, or basin that holds water; in the cave, hut, or house that, like the womb, offers shelter from storm and flood, heat and cold. Later, as civilizations developed, this symbolism of the body of the goddess was extended to include any enclosed area such as a forest glade, a temple precinct, a cathedral or church, a city, a house, a walled garden; any place that offered sanctuary and shelter. The symbolism of the vessel is extended to the ship that, like a mother with her child, carries its passengers across the sea of life.

HOPE *George Frederick Watts* 1817–1904

Then there are all the images of food and nourishment that have always belonged
to the mythology of the Great Mother. The Tree of Life stands at the root of this
chain of images. The Tree in many cultures was sacred to the goddess, standing in the
precincts of her temples in Sumer and Egypt, India and China, a symbolic offering of
her abundant life for the nourishment of all her children. Demeter and Ceres are the
last goddesses in the West to remind us of this ancient connection between the Great
Mother, the earth, and all the food the earth offers us in the way of sustenance.
Patriarchal religions seem to have lost the image of the earth as a Mother who
provides humanity with food. Nor do they have, as Egypt, Sumer, India, and China
had, an image of the Divine Feminine who provides the soul with the food of
eternal life.

Flowers are the most exquisite images of nature's power to delight us with her
beauty. The lily and the rose, whose scent intoxicates and whose perfection of form
invites love and awe, seem always to have belonged with the image of the goddess. In
Egypt and the East, it was the lotus that was offered at her shrines.

Jewels and precious metals, mined in the labyrinthine passages of the earth's
womb, are symbols of the hidden treasures buried within the soul, in the substratum
of our lives. They have always been sacred to the Great Mother. Silver, in particular,
was "her" metal, because it belonged to the night world ruled by the moon.

Woman's experience of being the carrier and nurturer of life, living, as it were, the
role of the Great Mother, bound to the greater rhythm of nature by the rhythms of
her menstrual cycle and the ten lunar months of gestation before the birth of her
child, has given a profound value, meaning, and responsibility to her life. The
observation through countless millennia of the way women carried their children in
the womb, gave birth to them, nourished and cared for them during their dependent
years, endowed women with a numinous significance as the carrier of life and as the
guardian of the plants, trees, and crops she tended in the Paleolithic and Neolithic
eras. In some cultures today, she still fills this ancient role.

YGGDRASIL,
THE NORSE
TREE OF LIFE

The Divine Feminine, whether as nature without or within, has a beneficent, nurturing, supportive aspect but also a destructive, abandoning, dissolving one. The "terrible" aspect of the goddess is documented in almost every early mythology. The powerlessness of humanity in the face of nature's terrifying power to destroy everything that it has built up is deeply imprinted on the memory of the race. Everything that can destroy life in a few brief moments is carried in the image of nature as the "terrible mother" who abandons and destroys her children or inflicts suffering on them. Fate has always been imagined as a goddess.

All these symbols of the Feminine are important, just as the symbols of the Masculine are important, for an understanding of ourselves and our dreams, for it is in dreams that the soul speaks to us in the preverbal language of symbols. How are we to create a relationship with this unseen dimension if we don't understand the symbolic language it uses to communicate with us?

The soul carries within it the active intelligence, the intention, and the power to transform these unconscious patterns so that humanity can reach its evolutionary goal of a complete, transformed consciousness. It communicates with us through all these images and many more, trying to make us aware of its existence, trying to create a relationship with us, but we, knowing nothing of this dimension, let the messages pass unnoticed. Sometimes the soul takes the form of a goddess, an old woman, a terrifying witch, trying to tell us what is happening beyond the level of the conscious mind. Sometimes the form she takes is so powerful that we cannot assimilate its meaning but can only live with the image, allowing it to transform us over many years. Becoming familiar with all these symbolic images and discovering, through insight into their meaning, how to bring mind and soul into relationship, harmony, and balance, could change our beliefs, our lives, and our culture.

CHAPTER THREE

MOTHER EARTH

Native Traditions

> *Holy Mother Earth, the trees, and all
> nature are witnesses to your thoughts
> and deeds.*
>
> WINNEBAGO WISE SAYING

Nothing is as important for the recovery of the feminine face of God as a rich and reverent understanding of the traditions of the world's First Peoples. In them is preserved our original human relationship with Mother Earth in all her wisdom, humility, and divine radiance.

The songs, myths, rituals, and living customs of those native peoples who have preserved their truth against huge odds speak to us of the grandeur of earth, of the wonders of nature, of the mysterious and marvelous ways in which Mother Earth surrounds, sustains, and instructs us at every moment.

In listening humbly to the traditions of these native peoples, we remember who we once were and what we still can be; we can experience once again the naked divine truth of the natural world and can learn from that experience to respect the laws of nature.

A FEMALE SHAMAN
FROM KRASNOYARSK

And what do the native traditions tell us of human and natural life if we listen? They initiate us into the three laws of sacred feminine reality – the Law of Unity, the Law of Rhythm, and the Law of the Love of the Dance. Taken together these three "laws" oppose to our fragmented, exploitative, self-obsessed forms of knowing and living an entirely different, far richer, and saner vision of what it is to be human and divine, and alive in nature.

Read what survives of the myths, songs, and rituals of any tribal peoples – whether the Inuit from Greenland, the Kogis from Colombia, or the Navaho from North America – and what will be immediately apparent is the knowledge running through them that life is one: one energy, one power, one force. Historians of religion used to believe that monotheism started with Akhenaten and the Jews; but the understanding of the sacredness of unity behind multiplicity was already alive in those tribal traditions that see life as one and everything that lives as holy. According to native traditions all living things are related to everything else, in a web of extraordinary delicacy that stretches over the whole universe. All things are in this web and part of it, and everything done to one of the parts of the web is done to all of the others. What the Mahayana Buddhist mystics call interdependence (or more fashionably "interbeing") is as old as the Aborigine's understanding that the rock formations of their deserts were "lines" in a song the Divine World was trying to "sing" to them; as old as the Inuit's knowledge that before seals could be hunted, the Ancestor Seal and the Gods of Nature must be prayed to; as old as the Native American's honoring of the buffalo after they killed it. Native traditions offer us a passionate awareness of this "interbeing." For them there is nothing sophisticated or intellectual about it; it is as obvious as sunlight or the cry of a baby. Reexperiencing the world in this unmediated intensity of connection is crucial to the recovery of the Divine Feminine. Unless we recover the primal poetry of the Law of Unity with all things, we will go on killing and exploiting in a frenzy of false separation from nature and so from our deep selves, and we will continue to ruin our world.

The second law that native traditions, wherever they come from, all honor is the Law of Rhythm. Living in naked reliance on nature inevitably entails a reverence for those rhythmic cycles that permeate the whole of nature's workings. The laws of nature and so of the human life that is everywhere sustained by nature's environment are rhythmic. Our hearts contract and then swell out as they suck in and pump our blood; spring follows summer and winter precedes spring; the brain is swept by endless wavelike pulses of sleep, wakefulness, hunger, satiation. Only by recapturing – and following – this sense of life's rhythms will we be able to survive. Opening to the law of rhythm requires developing feminine powers of imagination, attention, receptivity, capacity to wonder, nurture, and cherish, and a constantly, acutely sensitive, and sensible down-to-earth subtlety of approach that attempts to mirror the suppleness of life itself and its rhythmic alternations. If we wish to heal the natural world that we are in imminent danger of destroying, we are going to have to rebuild in ourselves those inner senses that can listen in radical humility to its voices, attend to its rhythms, and enact quickly what they tell us.

NORTH AMERICAN INDIANS' FERTILITY RITES *Nicholas de Bry* 16th century

The third law of the Divine Feminine that native traditions initiate us into, if we let them, is the Law of the Love of the Dance. What is astonishing, when you read what has come down to us of the tribal myths and songs, is that despite the knowledge they all have of life and nature's horrors and difficulties, they ring with praise and adoration and gratitude for the blessing of being alive on the earth. In so doing, they give all contemporary seekers of the Divine Feminine, a very clear vision of that living in intimacy with nature the Mother necessitates – and creates – and what a return of that life-wisdom means. The restoration of the Divine Feminine to the heart and mind of the world will mean a return to the type of passionate embrace of life in all its pain, wildness, and passion that we see in tribal traditions. The native peoples never make any separation between soul and body, heart and mind, prayer and action, the "other world" and this one. They did not make these separations, not because they aren't capable of doing so, as certain arrogant modern thinkers have claimed, but because they would have seen such separations as crazy, as a betrayal of the unity of all being. Realizing this unity of being gives native peoples a rugged, unshakable faith in life's goodness. Within tribal traditions being born a human is to be born into a dance that every animate or inanimate, visible or invisible being is also dancing. Every step of this dance is printed in light, its energy is adoration, its rhythm is praise.

The health of so vibrant a wisdom depends on it not being in the slightest sentimental. People like the Aborigines who live in the naked exposure to desert, or like the Siberians or the Tibetans who know the rigors of the tundra or the mountains, have no room or need for sentiment. What they live is reality without mask, and what they discover in this full-hearted living of reality is that pain, desolation, and destruction are not separate from the Great Dance but essential energies of its transformative unfolding. Death itself can never unnerve or destroy this dance; death after all is the life-spring of its fabulous and endless fertility, the Mother of all its changing magnificence. This tremendous YES to life is the YES of the

THE INDIAN WIDOW *Joseph Wright of Derby 1734–1797*

Divine Feminine, the YES that we must all find again within our deepest hearts if we are really going to fight together to preserve the planet.

Alongside and intimately interwoven with these three sacred laws inherent in native traditions is that radical humility that comes from accepting incarnation. This humility of being embodied and of accepting the terms and responsibilities is essential to the recovery of the feminine face of God. When Oren Lyons, chief of the Onondaaga Indians, addressed the United Nations in 1977, he said, "I do not see

NAVAJO COSMIC COUPLE: EARTH MOTHER, SKY FATHER

here a delegate for the eagles." He was not being witty; he was pointing to the essence of his tribal wisdom and what it had to communicate. Because life is one rhythmic, sacred dance, everything that is alive deserves to – and must – be listened to, respected, and honored. Even more radically, Lyons was implying that everything that lives – whether whale or ladybug, human being or eagle – is in some fundamental mystical sense EQUAL. Such a wisdom seems laughable to those who have been trained on several millennia of invisible hierarchy-building, but it corresponds exactly to the outrageous Mother-vision of a Ramakrishna or a St. Francis and all other beings whom Love has sprung free of the prison of anthropomorphic self-importance and the desire for power. Oren Lyons goes on to say that humankind's greatness lies in the human being's capacity to come into true humble relation with all things in the Sacred and so assume the full and noble responsibility for guardianship under God of the Creation – a guardianship that is never, under any circumstances, a license to exploit or destroy any other beings, except for food or in legitimate defense of territory. Unless we all recover this radical humility – perhaps the greatest gift of the Divine Feminine – and with it this vision of guardianship-in-reverence, the planet will not be preserved. Living in unity with nature can give us, as it gave the First Peoples, a sanely and soberly ecstatic vision of what and who we are, a vision whose balance is essential for our survival.

EARTH TEACH ME TO REMEMBER

Earth teach me stillness
   as the grasses are stilled with light.
Earth teach me suffering
   as old stones suffer with memory.
Earth teach me humility
   as blossoms are humble
   with beginning.
Earth teach me caring
   as the mother who secures
   her young.
Earth teach me courage
   as the tree which stands all alone.
Earth teach me limitation
   as the ant which crawls on
   the ground.
Earth teach me freedom
   as the eagle which soars in the sky.
Earth teach me resignation
   as the leaves which die in the fall.
Earth teach me regeneration
   as the seed which rises in the
   spring.
Earth teach me to forget myself
   as melted snow forgets its life.
Earth teach me to remember kindness
   as dry fields weep with rain.

THE UTE OF NORTH AMERICA

NORSE SPIRIT OF THE SEA

A HYMN TO THE MOTHER

In the beginning
   there was blackness.
Only the sea.
In the beginning there was no sun,
   no moon, no people.
In the beginning there were
   no animals, no plants.
Only the sea.
The sea was the Mother.
The Mother was not the people,
   she was not anything.
Nothing at all.
She was when she was, darkly.

THE KOGIS OF SOUTH AMERICA

THE inhabitant or soul of the
universe is never seen; its voice alone is
heard…It has a gentle voice like a
woman, a voice so fine and gentle that
even children cannot become afraid.
What it says is, "Be not afraid of the
universe."

ALASKAN SAYING

SONG TO ALA

Goddess of the
Ibo people of Africa

Holy Mother Earth
She who guides those who live upon Her,
She whose laws the people of the Ibo follow,
living in the honesty and rightness
that are the ways of Goddess Ala;
it is She who brings the child to the womb
and She who gives it life,
always present during life
and receiving those whose lives are ended,
taking them back into Her sacred womb,
"the pocket of Ala."

BEHOLD OUR MOTHER EARTH

BEHOLD! Our Mother Earth
 is lying here.
Behold! She gives of her fruitfulness.
Truly, her power she gives us.
Give thanks to Mother Earth
 who lies here.

Behold on Mother Earth the
 growing fields!
Behold the promise of her fruitfulness!
Truly, her power she gives us.
Give thanks to Mother Earth
 who lies here.

Behold on Mother Earth the
 spreading trees!
Behold the promise of her fruitfulness!
Truly, her power she gives us.
Give thanks to Mother Earth
 who lies here.

Behold on Mother Earth the
 running streams!
We see the promise of her fruitfulness.
Truly, her power she gives us.
Our thanks to Mother Earth
 who lies here.

THE PAWNEE OF NORTH AMERICA

HINA THE MEDIATRIX, MITIGATOR OF MANY THINGS

After the creation, peace and harmony everywhere existed for a long time. But at last, discontentment arose and there was war among the gods in their different regions, and among men, so Ta'aroa and Tu [male divinities] uttered curses to punish them.

They cursed the stars, which made them blink; and they cursed the moon, which caused it to wane and go out. But Hina [the First Woman], the mitigator of many things, saved their lives. Since then, the host of stars are ever bright, but keep on twinkling; and the moon always returns after it disappears.

They cursed the sea, which caused low tide; but Hina preserved the sea, which produced high tide; and so these tides have followed each other ever since.

They cursed the rivers, which frightened away the water, so that they hid beneath the soil; but Hina reproduced the shy waters, which formed springs, and so they continue to exist.

TAHITI, POLYNESIA

ASA BAZHONOODAH

THE earth is our mother. The white man is ruining our mother. I don't know the white man's ways, but to us the Mesa, the air, the water, are Holy Elements. We pray to these Holy Elements in order for our people to flourish and perpetuate the well-being of each generation...

The whites have neglected and misused the Earth. Soon the Navajo will resemble the Anasazi ruins. The wind took them away because they misused the Earth.

The white men wish that nothing will be left to us after this is over. They want us like the Anasazi.

Who likes it, nobody likes it, everybody has something to do with it.

Our Mother is being scarred.

CHIEF SEATTLE'S CREED

Every part of this earth is sacred to my people. Every shining pine needle, every sandy shore, every mist in the dark woods, every meadow, every humming insect. All are holy in the memory and experience of my people. We know the sap that courses through the tree as we know the blood that courses through our veins. We are part of the earth and it is part of us. The perfumed flowers are our sisters. The bear, the deer, the great eagle, these are our brothers. The rocky crests, the juices in the meadows, the body heat of the pony, and man, all belong to the same family. The shining water that moves in the stream and river is not just water but the blood of our ancestors…Will you teach your children what we have taught our children? That the earth is our mother? What befalls the earth, befalls all the sons of the earth. This we know: the earth does not belong to man, man belongs to the earth. All things are connected like the blood that connects us all. Man does not weave the web of life, he is merely a strand in it. Whatever he does to the web, he does to himself.

CHIEF SEATTLE, 1855

THE UNIVERSAL MOTHER

The mother of our songs, the mother of all our seed, bore us in the beginning of things and so she is the mother of all types of men, the mother of all nations. She is the mother of the thunder, the mother of the streams, the mother of the trees and all things. She is the mother of the world and of the older brothers, the stone people. She is the mother of the fruits of the earth and of all things. She is the mother of our youngest brothers, the French, and the strangers. She is the mother of our dance paraphernalia, of all our temples, and she is the only mother we possess. She alone is the mother of the fire and the Sun and the Milky Way…She is the mother of the rain and the only mother we possess. And she has left us a token in all temples…a token in the form of songs and dances.

THE KAGABA OF SOUTH AMERICA

FUJI

Guardian of the Fire
upon the blazing mountain
that stands not far from ancient Yedo,
Her sacred throne floats in the flames
so that all may know of Her
     sovereign power,
of Her sacred place upon the
     Eternal Mountain,
towering rock that touches earth as it
     touches heaven,
as Fuji looks upon Her own beauty
in the mirror surface of the lakes
that lay about Her feet.

Some say that She descended from
     the heavens
as the woman Tureh who lived upon
     Mount Fuji,
first woman of the world
who brought the knowledge of existence
to those on earth,
for though it is the mighty Goddess Fuji

who governs from the mountain of flame,
it is Her daughter who is the spirit
     of the hearth,
the one who taught of warmth
     from the cold,
the one who taught of the fire
     beneath the pot.

Ancestress of the once mighty Ainu people,
was it She who lived as Mother Bear,
great white furry being
who lived upon the guiding light
     that never moved
from the ancient Ainu home in heaven,
polar star where souls may rest
before returning once again to earth?
Each year, at the time of the Iyomande,
the messenger cub was sent to heaven
by those who lived in the caves
upon the islands that floated in the waters,
to remind the Mother of the constant star
that they would one day return home.

PRAISE POEM
TO OSHUN

Goddess of the Yoruba
people of Africa

Brass and parrot feathers
on a velvet skin
White cowrie shells
on black buttocks.
Her eyes sparkle in the forest,
like the sun on the river.
She is the wisdom of the forest
she is the wisdom of the river.
Where the doctor failed
she cures with fresh water.
Where medicine is impotent
she cures with fresh water
She cures the child
and does not charge the father.
She feeds the barren woman with
    honey
and her dry body swells up
like a juicy palm fruit
Oh, how sweet
is the touch of the child's hand.

✳

HYMN TO KUNAPIPI

First Mother of the
Aborgines of Australia

Dear Kunapipi,
Great Kunapipi,
I do not forget you
as I climb back into your holy womb
to make contact with my spirit soul,
crawling into the crescent vessel
of your protection
dug deep into the soil of your body,
carved into the precious earth beneath me.
I beckon to my spirit soul
which lives within you
until my time of finishing this life
and though I leave your womb
at this initiation time,
though I choose to climb out
from your nurturing warmth,
to live my years of life,
I ask you to care for my spirit soul
until my return
so that after my passing from this life
my two spirits may be reunited in you,
before you send me forth again
to once more live on earth.
Dear Kunapipi,
no matter how far I wander,
how many lives I live —
to you I shall always return.

CHASM OF THE COLORADO   *Thomas Moran* 1837–1926

ATHAPASCAN LEGEND
FROM WESTERN CANADA

When Mother Earth was very young, the mountains and the rivers of Her proud body blossomed in the springtime of Her being. She was more than fair to look upon, but Her greatest beauty of all was that part of Her that became the homeland of the Northern Athapascan peoples...

It was on this most perfect part of Earth that Asintmah, first woman of the world, appeared at the foot of Mount Atiksa near the Athabasca River. The holy Asintmah walked among the forests that grew upon Earth, gathering branches that had been discarded by the trees, careful not to tear or wrench away any that might still be growing on the body of the Earth. Joining these branches together, Asintmah built the first loom. And upon it she wove the fibers of the fireweed, the willow herb that Earth so favored, weaving them into The Great Blanket of Earth.

Once the weaving was completed, Asintmah began her long walk to spread the sacred blanket across the vast body of Earth. Then sitting down beside the edge of the blanket, Asintmah began to weave threads of music, singing of all the beauties of Earth, singing songs of how Earth would soon give birth to new lives, beings as perfect as Herself...

Suddenly all was quiet. Earth lay still and calm once again. It was in this way that Asintmah knew that the children born of Earth's womb had been delivered...So it was that with the help of the holy Asintmah, the woman who existed before all others, Maiden Earth became Mother Earth. And although this all happened a very long time ago, Athapascan people remember that even now they must care for their aging mother, the one who gave them life, and honor the memory of the woman Asintmah who was with Her in the beginning.

CHAPTER FOUR

TREE OF LIFE

Ancient Egypt

She is the Lady of Heaven, Earth, and the Netherworld,
Having brought them into existence through what her heart
conceived and her hands created.

HYMN IV, TEMPLE OF PHILAE
FROM *Hymns to Isis in Her Temple at Philae* BY L. ZABKAR

*L*uminous, nurturing, awesome, compassionate, the voice of the Divine Feminine speaks from the heart of Egyptian culture, bringing from the Neolithic era the image of the whole of life as a divine unity. The goddesses in Egypt were the Tree of Life – the date palm and the sycamore tree with its milky sap – and were often shown as the tree, offering from its leafy interior vases that contained the water of eternal life, nourishment for the souls passing from one dimension to another.

Among the ancient Egyptian goddesses of greatest influence was Maat, who wore on her head the ostrich feather against which each human heart was weighed after death, balanced on the scales of justice. Maat is perhaps the origin of the figure of Divine Wisdom in the Old Testament, for she personified the equilibrium and harmony of the universe intrinsic to all life forms, even to the notes of the musical

HATHOR PLACES
THE MAGIC COLLAR
ON SETHI I
19th Dynasty
1314–1200 B.C.

scale. She was the music of life, the principle of Divine Order, Truth, and Harmony, which is embodied in Natural Law. But each goddess was an aspect of the pulse of life emanating from the hidden source of all. Together with their consorts, the gods, they gave Egypt the structure and organization and creative dynamism that were grounded in a profound feeling for the sacredness of life and the certainty that everything was ensouled with divine presence.

Some of the most beautiful hymns and prayers that have come down to us were addressed to Nut as Mother of the souls of the dead. Nut, goddess of the starry night sky, whose hieroglyph was the water jar, was the deep ground of life and of the soul. Her image was painted on the inside of the coffin, sometimes on the base as well as the lid, as if to enfold the soul entrusted to her care in her maternal embrace.

Hathor was Egypt's oldest goddess who, with Isis, was closest to the people. At times, Hathor was the nurturing Mother of the universe. At others, she was the creative impulse flowing from the great ocean of space, the womb or ground of being. In this form as primary creator, like the god Ptah in Memphis, everything that she imagined or conceived in her heart instantly became manifest. At the same time, in the great temples raised to her at Memphis, Thebes, and Dendara, the people felt her close to them, her maternal presence immanent within the forms of creation, residing in her sanctuary at the temple's heart. Her divine number was seven.

A legend, in which Hathor may have been imagined as the Milky Way – the Divine Cow Mother – said that in her cosmic form she gave birth to the sun and carried it between her horns as she swam in the ocean of her divine being. The rain-milk, flowing like a flood from her udders, nourished and sustained the whole earth. Sometimes Hathor is shown in her cow form standing at the entrance to the mountain of the dead, receiving the souls of the dead back into herself. Her belly became the star-spangled night sky, and the four cardinal points of the universe were fixed where her four legs touched the earth. Another legend said that the sun and moon were her eyes and sometimes she was called "Mother of the Light." Like Isis,

ISIS PROTECTS THE SHRINE OF TUTANKHAMUN WITH HER WINGS
18th Dynasty

she was worshiped as the brilliant star Sothis or Sirius whose dawn rising, like a golden lotus, heralded the regenerating flood of the Nile.

The people loved and worshiped Hathor as life's magnetic, fertilizing energy, which attracts people and animals to each other and manifests as the fertility of earth. They saw her as radiantly beautiful like the sun, but they also feared her as the bringer of the parching heat of summer and death, disease, and war. In her form as Sekhmet, the awesome lion-headed goddess whose name means "The Powerful One," she could withhold the water of life, inflicting drought and starvation. Yet, although she could bring destruction, she could also reverse or set limits to what she had done, so she was always shown wearing the *menat*, the sacred necklace of healing,

A GODDESS DISTRIBUTES THE FOOD
AND DRINK OF IMMORTALITY
13th century B.C.

and holding the *sistrum*, the musical rattle with her face on it, which banished the forces of evil. Hathor was the impulse to love, the outpouring of joy and beauty. She was the boundless fecundity of life that was later reflected in the goddess Aphrodite in Greece. Music, dance, poetry, and song were her gifts. Lovers appealed to her for her blessing and help in attracting their beloved. At night her temples were filled with the music of flute, harp, and tambourine as her devotees expressed their love for her in dance and song. One hymn to her says, "The nourishment of thy heart is dance."

Isis, sister and wife of Osiris and mother of the falcon-headed sun god Horus, was worshiped for over three thousand years, from predynastic times (before 3000 B.C.) to well into Roman times (second century A.D.) when temples were raised to her throughout the Roman Empire. With the coming of Christianity, her shrines were rededicated to the Virgin Mary.

Virgin Mother of all life, yet mother and wife on earth, Isis was worshiped as the Immortal Goddess, the One who brings the many into being, the feminine aspect of the primeval abyss from which all life came. For all her many roles, she took the names of different goddesses. But her names and titles do not convey the people's love for her, nor the depth of their need for her and their trust in her, nor the influence she had on Egyptian civilization for over three thousand years. In relation to the pharaoh, the ruler of Egypt, she was the Cosmic Mother, the lap or throne on which he sat as her "son," who bestowed on him his right to rule and the divine qualities and powers of kingship.

There is an immense range of thought and feeling that the image of Isis carries, for, in the people's imagination, she filled many mythological roles. Besides her cosmic dimension as the Great Mother (God-Mother), she was the supreme image of a wife and mother on earth. Isis was both goddess and woman, both divine and human. As Queen of Heaven she was the regent of the stars and the one who placed them in orbit and was worshiped as the star Sothis (Sirius), whose rising with the sun after a seventy-day absence announced the inundation of the Nile. At times she merged with Hathor and was the milk-giving Divine Cow, nourisher and sustainer of the universe. As Queen of Earth, she was the fertility of the earth's life, "The Green One" or "The Creator of Green Things." As Queen of the Underworld she was, with her husband Osiris, one of the judges of the dead, and the wind of her great wings as the vulture goddess, Nekhbet, gave them the breath of eternal life. These wings, so wonderfully painted on the walls of Queen Nefertari's tomb, appear again wrapped protectively around the sarcophagus of Tutankhamun. As the Tree of Life, Isis, like Nut and Hathor, offered the food and water of immortality to the dead.

The Egyptians celebrated myth because it kept them in touch with the Mystery of the Invisible that was carried by the images of their goddesses and gods. The great myth that tells the story of Isis's search for Osiris is a lunar one, a story of darkness and light, of death and rebirth. Osiris was the brother and the husband of Isis, and they had a brother, Seth, who was jealous of him and who twice arranged his murder. At a great banquet held in honor of Osiris, Seth invited him to climb into a casket he had had specially made to fit him. Abruptly shutting the lid and trapping Osiris inside it, he had it thrown into the Nile, where it floated north to Byblos on the Phoenician coast. Isis set out in search of Osiris and miraculously found the casket with him lying in it. Taking the form of a large bird, a kite, she fanned him to life with the beating of her great wings and in this form, conceived their child Horus. But Seth found the casket and, while Isis was away with Horus, hacked Osiris's body into fourteen pieces, scattering them throughout Egypt. Isis again set out in search of her husband and, finding the pieces of his body, brought them all together and once again restored him to life by fanning him with her wings.

This myth was performed each year in the temple of Osiris at Abydos and in Isis's temple at Philae. Her role in the myth carries the message (later reaffirmed in the Greek myth of Demeter and Persephone) that the universe as Mother cares for the life she has brought into being and has the power to overcome death. It was Isis's devotion to Osiris, her untiring quest for the scattered fragments of his dismembered body, that made possible his resurrection from the dead. It was the tears of Isis weeping for the murdered Osiris that helped to restore him to life and made the waters of the Nile swell into the great flood that nourished the land of Egypt and brought forth the green shoots of the reborn Osiris. Like Demeter in Greece, Isis brings the divine down to earth, showing human devotion, human grief and anguish, human courage and unwearying tenacity in her quest to find her husband and restore him to life. It was the passionate love of Isis for Osiris that made her so beloved a goddess of the Egyptian people.

In the time of one of Egypt's late rulers, Ptolemy II (284–246 B.C.), a series of wonderful hymns addressed to Isis were inscribed in hieroglyphs on the walls of her temple at Philae, in southern Egypt. Only recently translated, they offer a complete vision of how the Egyptians saw her, for the priest or priests who wrote them drew on much older material as the basis of their hymns. At this temple Isis gathered to herself as "Lady of Life" and "Lady of Upper and Lower Egypt" all the roles, attributes, and functions of the other great goddesses of Egypt. For the people, she was their Mother, dwelling in the dimension of the divine yet at the same time close to them in her sanctuary on earth.

THE GODDESSES ISIS AND NEPHTHYS STAND BEHIND
OSIRIS IN HIS SHRINE OF FIRE

Creator of the universe and sustainer of its life, she descended daily to her
sanctuary to become one with her golden image and render the place holy by her
presence. Like Hathor, she was called "The Golden One." Her image, covered with
gold leaf and dimly lit by two small shafts, gleamed in the dim light of her sanctuary,
which seemed to be "filled with gold, like the horizon supporting the sun-disc." Each
day, her statue was anointed with fragrant oils and perfumes and with myrrh. Papyrus
flowers and the sacred blue lotus were laid before her. She filled the space with her
radiance, and those who came to worship or to implore her help trembled in awe
and longing before her.

HYMN TO NUT

GREAT one, who became Heaven,
Thou didst assume power;
    thou didst stir;
Thou hast filled all places
    with thy beauty.
The whole earth lies beneath thee.
Thou has taken possession of it.
Thou enclosest the earth
    and all things in thy arms.

FROM *Kingship and the Gods*
BY H. FRANKFORT

HYMN TO HATHOR

All hail, jubilation to you,
    O Golden One,
Sole ruler, Uraeus of the Supreme
    Lord himself!
Mysterious one, who gives birth to the
    divine entities, forms the animals, models
    them as she pleases, fashions men...
O Mother!...Luminous One who thrusts
    back the darkness,
Who illuminates every human creature
    with her rays,
Hail Great One of many names...

FROM *Egyptian Mysteries* BY L. LAMY

HYMN TO ISIS

O ISIS, the Great, God's Mother,
    Lady of Philae,
God's Wife, God's Adorer, and
    God's Hand,
God's Mother and Great Royal Spouse,
Adornment and Lady of the
    Ornaments of the Palace.

Lady and desire of the green fields,
Nursling who fills the palace [temple]
    with her beauty,
Fragrance of the palace, mistress of joy,
Who completes her course in the
    Divine Place.

Rain-cloud that makes green the fields
    when it descends,
Maiden, sweet of love, Lady of Upper
    and Lower Egypt,
Who issues orders among the
    divine Ennead,
According to whose command
    one rules.

Princess, great of praise, lady of charm,
Whose face enjoys the trickling of
    fresh myrrh.

HYMN III, TEMPLE OF PHILAE
FROM *Hymns to Isis in Her Temple at Philae*
BY L. ZABKAR

HYMN TO HATHOR

Oh! how beautiful!
The Gold is radiant!
The Gold is radiant, shining, radiant!
For you the sky and the stars
    strike the tambourine
the sun and the moon adore you,
    the gods revere you
and the goddesses sing you hymns.

Oh! how beautiful!
The Gold is radiant!
The Gold is radiant, shining, radiant!
For you the whole earth
    strikes the tambourine
and everything that is in it
    dances for you,
The Double-Land and the foreign
    lands revere you for you placed the
    sky on its four supports...

Oh! how beautiful!
The Gold is radiant!
The Gold is radiant, shining, radiant!
For you men and women
    strike the tambourine.
The Divine-Powers, the stars,
    dance for you.
The Double-Land, ecstatic,
    reveres you.
The two uraeus make gestures of
    praise to you.

FROM *Hymnes et Prières de l'Egypte Ancienne*
BY A. BARUCQ AND F. DUMAS
TRANSLATED BY ANNE BARING

HYMN TO NUT

O GREAT Being who is in
    the world of the Dead,
At whose feet is Eternity,
In whose hand is the Always,
    Come to me.
O Great Divine Beloved Soul,
Who is in the mysterious abyss,
    Come to me.

FROM AN INSCRIPTION IN THE LOUVRE

HYMN TO ISIS

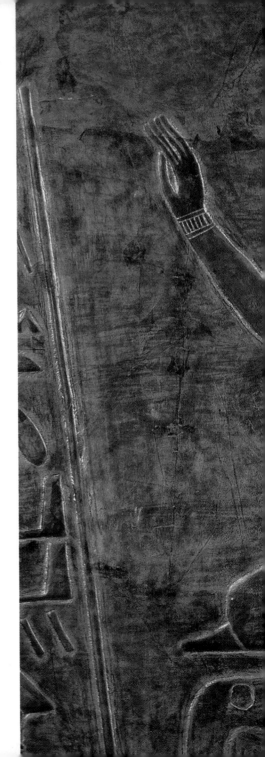

Isis, giver of life, residing in the
    Sacred Mound, Satis,
Lady of Biggeh:
She is the one who pours out
    the Inundation
That makes all people live and
    green plants grow,
Who provides divine offerings for the gods,
And invocation-offerings for
    the Transfigured ones.

Because she is the Lady of Heaven,
Her man [Osiris] is the
    Lord of the Netherworld,
Her son [Horus] is the Lord of the Land;
Her man is the pure water, rejuvenating
    himself at Biggeh at his time.

She is the Lady of Heaven, Earth,
    and the Netherworld
Having brought them into existence
    through what her heart
conceived and her hands created...

HYMN IV, TEMPLE OF PHILAE
FROM *Hymns to Isis in Her Temple at Philae*
BY L. ZABKAR

RELIEF OF ISIS FROM
THE TOMB OF PRINCESS YI

HYMN TO ISIS

I PLAY the sistra before
   your beautiful face,
Isis, Giver of Life, residing in
   the Sacred Mound,
Eye of Re who has no equal
   in heaven and on earth.
Great of love, mistress of women,
who fills heaven and earth with
   her beauty...

HYMN VII, TEMPLE OF PHILAE
FROM *Hymns to Isis in Her
Temple at Philae*
BY L. ZABKAR

HYMN TO NUT

O my mother Nut,
Stretch your wings over me,
Let me become like the
   imperishable stars,
Like the indefatigable stars —
May Nut extend her arms over me
And her name of
"She who extends her arms,
Chases away the shadows,
And makes the Light shine
   everywhere."

FROM AN INSCRIPTION ON
A COFFIN LID IN THE LOUVRE

OSIRIS WAS BROUGHT BACK TO LIFE BY ISIS
1st century B.C.

ISIS AND HER SISTER NEPHTHYS

A VISION OF ISIS

In the second century A.D., Lucius Apuleius, a devotee of Isis, had this great vision:
*The apparition of a woman began to rise from the middle of the sea with so lovely a
face that the gods themselves would have fallen down in adoration of it. First the
head, then the whole shining body gradually emerged and stood before me poised on
the surface of the waves...Her long thick hair fell in tapering ringlets on her lovely
neck, and was crowned with an intricate chaplet in which was woven every kind of
flower. Just above her brow shone a round disc, like a mirror, or like the bright face of
the moon, which told me who she was. Vipers rising from the left-hand and right-
hand partings of her hair supported this disc, with ears of corn bristling beside them.
Her many-colored robe was of finest linen; part was glistening white, part crocus-
yellow, part glowing red and along the entire hem a woven bordure of flowers and
fruit clung swaying in the breeze. But what caught and held my eye more than
anything else was the deep black luster of her mantle. She wore it slung across her
body from the right hip to the left shoulder, where it was caught in a knot resembling
the boss of a shield; but part of it hung in innumerable folds, the tasseled fringe
quivering. It was embroidered with glittering stars on the hem and everywhere else,
and in the middle beamed a full and fiery moon...On her divine feet were slippers of
palm leaves, the emblem of victory.*

Isis spoke to him, saying:

*I am Nature, the Universal Mother, mistress of all the elements, primordial child
of time, sovereign of all things spiritual, queen of the dead, queen also of the
immortals, the single manifestation of all gods and goddesses that are.
My nod governs the starry heights of Heaven, the wholesome sea-breezes,
the dreadful silence of the world below. Though I am worshiped in many aspects,
known by countless names, and propitiated with all manner of different rites, yet the
whole round earth venerates me.*

FROM L. APULEIUS, *The Golden Ass*
TRANSLATED BY ROBERT GRAVES

CHAPTER FIVE

COSMIC GODDESS

Sumer and Babylonia

I say, "Hail!" to Inanna, First daughter of the Moon!
Mighty, majestic and radiant,
You shine brilliantly in the evening,
You brighten the day at dawn.
You stand in the heavens like the sun and the moon,
Your wonders are known both above and below,
To the greatness of the holy priestess in heaven,
To you, Inanna, I sing!

FROM *Inanna, Queen of Heaven and Earth*
BY D. WOLKSTEIN AND S. M. KRAMER

𝒯he Divine Feminine in Sumer and Babylonia had many names, and our
understanding of the different goddesses and the roles they played is far from
complete. But it is clear that here, as in Egypt, life was imagined as coming forth
from the cosmos as Great Mother and that she was the nurturing and regenerating
power that sustained all creation. She was the water of life on which the people
depended for food, the terror of the raging storm, the dew-bringing moonlight, the

TERRACOTTA PLAQUE
OF INANNA–ISHTAR
c. 2300–2000 B.C.

warmth of the sun that ripened the wheat and barley. She was life and death. She was the immensity of cosmic space and the light of the great stars Venus and Sirius, which shone most brilliantly in the night sky and announced the dawn of a new day. As civilization was established, the goddess carried for the people the supreme values of the Divine Feminine: justice, wisdom, love, compassion. She presided over the laws of civilization, which reflected the divine laws of life embodied in the life of nature.

One hundred and fifty years ago, no one had heard of Inanna, the Great Goddess of Sumer. Nor was much known about Ishtar, Goddess of Babylonia, except through the writings of the Hebrew prophets who reviled her as "The Great Whore of Babylon." Even now, only a fragment of the immense body of cuneiform writings has been translated, so our knowledge about this ancient civilization is far from complete. Inanna's city – Uruk – where she was worshiped for over three thousand years has never been fully excavated. Yet only Egypt can rival the incalculable influence of Sumerian and Babylonian mythology on the sacred literature of later cultures and, in particular, its influence on the land of Canaan and the Hebrew culture that took root there.

Mesopotamia, subject to unpredictable and terrifying floods that could obliterate the labor of years in seconds, could not easily have built a sense of trust in its Great Mother. The biblical flood that brought death to almost the whole of humanity is an image that belongs to Mesopotamia rather than Egypt. The story of the flood passed from Sumerian and Babylonian to Hebrew mythology. In the earlier cultures, it is the goddess who laments the destruction of her people caused by the flood; yet in the Genesis version of the story, all trace of the goddess has vanished except for her birds: the raven and the dove. The harshness of the climate is reflected in the language, which does not lend itself easily to poetry but is stark, unadorned, conveying the immense and ambivalent power of nature to create and destroy life. Yet in this inhospitable desert, a garden of Eden was created through the genius of the Sumerians who, like the Egyptians, transformed the desert into flowering life.

SUMERIAN EARTH GODDESS
2000 B.C.

Each city had its goddess but there seem to have been certain goddesses who carried the image of the primordial Great Mother for the whole culture. There was Nammu, goddess of the heavenly waters and the great abyss of space – whose ideogram was the sea – and who may be the model for the Biblical image of Wisdom, she whose thoughts were more than the sea and whose counsels were profounder than the great deep (Sir. 24:29).

There was Ninhursag, the mother of the gods and of humanity who, like Hathor and Isis in Egypt, was the mother of the earth and all its plants and life-giving crops. She was also the mother of the wild animals and the herd animals: cow, sheep, and goat. Presiding over birth in all these different orders of creation, her ideogram – in the shape of a horseshoe – symbolized the womb, sheepfold, or cowbyre where life came into being. She was the generative power that gave shape to life in the womb; the dynamic agent that brought the fetus to birth; the heavenly midwife presiding over the birth of gods, mortals, and animals; the "Opener of the Womb." A sacred herd of cattle was always attached to her temple, and she was described, like Hathor and Isis in Egypt, as "The Great Cow," whose milk nourished all life on earth and all the people of Sumer.

But it was Inanna who was the best loved of the Sumerian goddesses, closest to the people's heart in the way Hathor and Isis were in Egypt. Inanna was the Great Goddess rather than the Great Mother of Sumer, imagined as a young and radiantly beautiful woman, daughter of the moon god. The emphasis is on the dynamism of her creative powers rather than on the nurturing qualities of a maternal role. She seems to be primarily a cosmic power, Queen of Heaven. In Babylonia and Assyria, she was called Ishtar. Farther to the west she was Astarte. As early as 4000 B.C. in Uruk, the principal site of her cult, Inanna was worshiped in her temple known as Eanna, or "The House of Heaven."

SUMERIAN CUNEIFORM WRITING
INSCRIBED TO INANNA
c. 2100 B.C.

The temple was described as being built of gold, silver, and lapis lazuli. Amazingly, in 500 B.C. she was still worshiped there, still shown riding in a chariot drawn by seven lions that symbolized perhaps the chariot and stars in the constellation of the Great Bear. Ishtar's reign in Babylon was nearly as long. The cult statues of both Inanna and Ishtar were splendidly dressed in wonderful robes and jewels of lapis lazuli and gold, and were carried through the streets and in boats on the great rivers on festival days. Lapis lazuli was "their" stone.

As Queen of Heaven, Inanna and Ishtar were adored as the crescent moon and as the morning and evening star we now call Venus and the great star Sirius that rose on the horizon with the sun. The Sumerians and Babylonians were fascinated by the stars. Nightly from their flat roofs and the terraces of their great temples they studied the patterns of the constellations as they wheeled overhead. They called the zodiacal belt the girdle of Ishtar and identified her with the constellation Virgo. The immense stellar river of the Milky Way may have inspired the title of "Great Cow" held by Inanna and Ishtar.

As Queen of Earth, the Great Goddess was the exuberant life of the grain and the vine, the date palm, cedar, sycamore, fig, olive, and apple tree. A tree, usually the sycamore, fig, or apple – the tree of life that was the goddess herself – always stood in the courtyards of their temples. The lapis lazuli walls of Ishtar's magnificent temple in Babylon were decorated with animals and trees. The goddess was called "The Green One," or "She of the Springing Verdure." In this role, she becomes nurturing mother, for all fruits and grain from the fields were the actual substance of her being, given for the nourishment of her "children." Special bread was made into "the cakes of the goddess Inanna," baked on her altars and offered to her – the offering of herself to herself. The harvested crop of the date palm, apple tree, and vine were the fruit of her womb. Foremost among the symbols of her power as Great Goddess were the caduceus, with its entwined snakes, the lion, and the owl. Inanna and Ishtar were both addressed as "Divine Lady Owl."

But there was another most important dimension to Inanna and Ishtar. As virgin goddesses, they both personified life's

ISHTAR, GODDESS OF BABYLONIA

oneness and its never-failing fecundity, its capacity endlessly to regenerate itself from an invisible source. Above all, they were the Goddess of Love and Sexual Desire. This cosmic energy was expressed on earth through sexual attraction. The power of the goddess was a most awesome aspect of her being – no creature, animal or human, was able to resist the urge to mate and therefore to create new life. Ishtar proclaimed: "I turn the male to the female; I am she who adorneth the male for the female; I am she who adorneth the female for the male." Sexual intercourse in the temple, where men came to sleep with the priestesses who were known as hierodules, or "servants of the holy," and where young women came to offer their virginity to the goddess, was a magical ritual that helped to increase the land's fertility and to circulate the creative energy flowing from the cosmic being of the goddess. It is hard for us who are so far from this kind of imaginal thinking to understand how these ancient peoples saw and felt the interconnectedness of everything. The Hebrew prophets were appalled by the licentiousness of Ishtar's rites in the Assyrian city of Babylon.

As in Egypt, the goddess was represented on earth by a high-priestess who was also a queen or princess. In the ritual of the sacred marriage, which took place annually in the autumn in Sumer, after the parching drought of summer had ended, the high-priestess took the role of the goddess in her sexual union with the king who personified the land of Sumer. It was the high-priestess as the goddess who bestowed kingship upon the ruler and who, as in Egypt, transmitted to him her cosmic power, her divine life force, so making him a mighty ruler.

Through the cuneiform script that has miraculously preserved her mythology, Inanna's names resonate and describe her many roles: Queen of Heaven and Earth, Priestess of Heaven, Holy Shepherdess, Light of the World, Righteous Judge, Framer of All Decrees, Forgiver of Sins, Opener of the Womb, Loud-thundering Storm, the Amazement of the Land, Wise One of Heaven. Above all, Inanna and Ishtar personified the radiance of starry light. Perhaps the most famous myth told about Inanna was "The Descent into the Netherworld," which was yearly enacted in the courtyards of her temples as a ritual of regeneration, just as the myth of Isis and Osiris was performed in the temples of Egypt. Ishtar had a similar myth, closer in imagery to the Egyptian one, which describes her descent into the underworld to awaken her son-lover Tammuz, so restoring fertility to the earth.

In Inanna's great myth, with its theme of the descent into darkness of the goddess who personified light, and her return, there is beauty, pathos, and compassion as well as cruelty, terror, and sacrifice. Inanna as Queen of Heaven makes her descent into the Netherworld, the dark domain of her sister Ereshkigal. As she descends she is forced to surrender her robes and her jewels and regalia of office at each of its seven gates until, naked and vulnerable, she is brought into the presence of its queen. Fixed by the goddess with the glance-that-can-kill, she is hung like a piece of meat on a hook. Following the lunar pattern of the myth, she hangs there for three days until she is rescued and brought back to life by emissaries sent by Enki, the God of Wisdom. She ascends into heaven, regaining at each gate her jewels, her luminous robes, and her royal powers.

Inanna is also known to us through an extraordinary series of poems addressed to her by a princess who was high-priestess of the temple of the moon god Nanna at Ur about 2300 B.C. As high-priestess, she became "the daughter" of the moon god and so the "sister" of Inanna who, in later Sumerian mythology, was Nanna's daughter. She was named Enheduanna and she was the daughter of King Sargon of Akkad. The power of that fierce father, the prototype of all future conquerors, vibrates in the words she uses to invoke Inanna, chilling the heart with their savage imagery. Enheduanna wrote three long poems in honor of Inanna: "Inanna and Ebeh," "Lady of Largest Heart," and "The Exaltation of Inanna." These are the earliest poems known to have been written by a woman and a high-priestess. For hundreds of years her hymns were sung in the temples of Inanna and Ishtar. In these poems Inanna personifies the ambivalent powers of nature as well as the process that transforms and regenerates. She is the wisdom embodied in the law that governs the movements of the stars as well as the cycles of life on earth. Cylinder seals show her riding on a dragon and holding a thunderbolt in her hand, and she is described as a dragon who spews forth the torrent of storm, flood, or war.

In these mythic poems, Inanna is exalted as Goddess of War, reflecting perhaps the dynastic ambitions of King Sargon. No poet has described more vividly the awesome cosmic power that can bring death as well as life. Enheduanna gave the kings who were later to identify themselves with the power of the Great Goddess a fearful model to follow. Almost two thousand years after Enheduanna, Ishtar, now Goddess of Assyria, says to a king, "In battle I fly like a swallow. I heap up heads that are so many harvested rushes...I will flay your enemies and present them to you." It is in this role that the goddess becomes degenerate, used to glorify war and condone human sacrifice.

The kings, whose sole aim was conquest, succumbed to a fatal inflation that drove them to inflict terrible suffering on the people of Mesopotamia. Ultimately, through

the increasing salinization of the land and the lust for war and barbaric cruelty of the Assyrians, so feared by the Hebrews, the great civilization died. The once flourishing land slowly returned to desert, burying the magnificent temples beneath the sand.

INANNA–ISHTAR AS GODDESS OF WAR

c. 2300 B.C.

This early poem shows the invisible presence of the Mother Goddess. Ki-Ninhursag is speaking:

Begetting Mother am I,
Within the Spirit I abide
And none see me.
In the word of An (father god) I abide
And none see me.
In the word of Enlil
(the son of An and Ki) I abide
And none see me.
In the word of the holy temple I abide,
And none see me.

FROM *Sumerian and Babylonian Psalms*
BY STEPHEN LANGDON

LADY OF LARGEST HEART

Your torch flames
heaven's four quarters
spreads splendorous light in the dark
you have realized
the Queen of Heaven and Earth
to the utmost
you hold everything
entirely in your hands
your storm-shot torrents drench the
    bare earth
moisten to life
moisture bearing light
floods the dark
O my Lady, my queen
I unfold your splendor in all lands
I extol your glory
I will praise your course
your sweeping grandeur forever.
Queen, Mistress
you are sublime
you are venerable
your great deeds
are boundless
may I praise
your eminence
O maiden Inanna
sweet is your praise

BY ENHEDUANNA
FROM *Inanna, Lady of Largest Heart*
BY B. DE SHONG MEADOR AND D. FOXVOG

THE LADY
OF THE EVENING

The Holy One stands all alone
in the clear sky;
Upon all the lands and upon
the black-haired people,
the people as numerous as sheep,
The Lady looks in sweet wonder
from heaven's midst;
They parade before the holy Inanna,
The Lady of the Evening,
Inanna, is lofty,
The Maid, Inanna, I would praise
as is fitting,
The Lady of the Evening is lofty
on the horizon.

FROM *The Poetry of Sumer*
BY S. M. KRAMER

THE HOLY
PRIESTESS OF HEAVEN

I SAY, "Hail!" to the Holy One who
appears in the heavens!
I say, "Hail!" to the Holy Priestess
of Heaven

Holy Torch! You fill the sky with Light!
You brighten the day at dawn!

I say "Hail!" to Inanna, Great Lady
of Heaven!
Awesome lady of the Annuna Gods!
Crowned with great horns,
You fill the heavens and the earth
with light!
I say, "Hail!" to Inanna, First daughter
of the Moon!

Mighty, majestic and radiant,
You shine brilliantly in the evening,
You brighten the day at dawn.
You stand in the heavens like the sun
and the moon,
Your wonders are known both above
and below,
To the greatness of the holy priestess
in heaven,
To you, Inanna, I sing!

FROM *Inanna, Queen of Heaven and Earth*
BY D. WOLKSTEIN AND S.M. KRAMER

THE LADY OF COMPASSION

She accepted the prayer
he had uttered,
The Queen of the searching eye,
the guide of the land,
the all-compassionate,
Removed from that man the bruising
cane that had been laid upon him,
Attacking on his behalf the demons of
disease and sickness, she extirpated
them from that man,
The whip that had been laid cruelly
upon him she made into
a cloth bandage,
She made the silver-ore as bright as
good silver, purified it,
She gazed upon him with joyous heart,
gave him life,
She returned him to the gracious hand
of his god,
Placed the ever-present good angels
at his head...
Blessed his womb, gave him an heir,
Gave him a spouse who bore him a
son, spread wide his stalls and
sheepfolds,
Gave him a faithful household,
decreed a sweet fate for him.

FROM *The Poetry of Sumer*
BY S. M. KRAMER

LADY OF LARGEST HEART

INANNA, child of the Moon God
A soft bud swelling
her queen's robe cloaks the slender
    stem
on her smooth brow she paints
fire beams and fearsome glint

fastens carnelian
blood-red and glowing
around her throat

and then her hand clasps
the seven-headed mace
she stands as in youth's prime
her right hand grasps the mace

steps, yes she steps her narrow foot
on the furred back
of a wild lapis lazuli bull

and she goes out
white-sparked, radiant
in the dark vault of evening's sky
star-steps in the street
through the Gate of Wonder.

BY ENHEDUANNA
FROM *Inanna, Lady of Largest Heart*
BY B. DE SHONG MEADOR AND D. FOXVOG

65

INANNA AND EBEH

Inanna! portentous one!
holy! ill-boding!
fury overturns her heart!

With screech of hinge
she flings wide the gate
of the house of battle

her hands pull the bolt lock
on its lapis lazuli door

bedlam unleashed
she sends down a raging battle
hurls a storm from her wide arms
to the ground below
thin sinew the woman strings
for her flawless arrows

and hurricane winds
swift-piercing, stinging,
fly with Inanna's fury
suck loosened earth into sweet air...

and her tongue's poison
hurls a green-wilting curse
over forest and fruit-bearing trees

she shows no mercy to its green
 plant rows
a parching drought she blows

dust dry air in her pitiless wake
gusts over stems of verdant growth
not a moist drop stays

in the bent and withered grass
she strikes fires
flames cut the sky to the
 boundary stones
flames dance in the smoke stained air
spread at a glance from the
 queen's glare.

BY ENHEDUANNA
FROM *Inanna, Lady of Largest Heart*
BY B. DE SHONG MEADOR AND D. FOXVOG

HYMN TO INANNA

LADY of all powers,
In whom light appears,
Radiant one
Beloved of Heaven and Earth,
Tiara-crowned
Priestess of the Highest God,
My Lady, you are the guardian
Of all greatness.
Your hand holds the seven powers:
You have hung them over your fingers,
You have gathered the many powers,
You have clasped them now
Like necklaces onto your breast.

BY ENHEDUANNA
FROM *Women in Praise of the Sacred*
BY JANE HIRSHFIELD

I beseech thee, Lady of ladies, Goddess of goddesses, Ishtar, queen of all cities, leader of all men. Thou art the Light of the World; thou art the Light of Heaven...Supreme is thy might, O Lady, exalted art thou above all gods. Thou renderest judgment and thy decision is righteous; unto thee are subject the laws of the earth and the laws of heaven, the laws of the temple and of the shrine, and the laws of the private apartment and of the secret chamber. Where is the place where thy name is not, and where is the spot where thy commandments are not known? At thy name the earth and the heavens shake, and the gods tremble; the spirits of heaven tremble at thy name and men hold it in awe. Thou art great, thou art exalted; all the men of Sumer, and all creatures, and all humanity glorify thy name. With righteousness dost thou judge the deeds of men, even thou; thou lookest upon the oppressed and to the downtrodden thou bringest justice every day. How long, Queen of Heaven and Earth, how long, Shepherdess of pale-faced men, wilt thou tarry? How long, Lady of Hosts, Lady of Battles? Glorious one whom all the spirits of heaven fear, who subduest all angry gods; mighty above all rulers, who holdest the reins of kings. Opener of the womb of all women, great is thy light. Shining light of heaven, light of the world, enlightener of all the places where men dwell, who gatherest together the hosts of the nations. Goddess of men, divinity of women, thy counsel passeth understanding. Where thou glancest the dead come to life and the sick rise and walk, and the mind that is distressed is healed when it looks upon thy face.

FROM *The Seven Tablets of Creation*
BY L.W. KING

CHAPTER SIX

GAIA

Ancient Greece

Gaia, mother of all
the foundation, the oldest one
I shall sing to Earth
She feeds everything that is in the world.

HOMERIC HYMN TO GAIA
FROM *The Myth of the Goddess*
TRANSLATED BY JULES CASHFORD

aia was the Great Mother of all life and Mother of the gods. Gaia was the earth, the foundation. She was "in the beginning." In Aeschylus's play, *The Eumenides*, the priestess at Delphi opens her invocation to the deities with the words, "First in my prayer before all other gods I call on Earth, primeval prophetess."

Today, as we awaken to the sacredness of our planetary home, the sacredness of earth that we were once instinctively aware of, the name and image of Gaia, the Great Mother, mysteriously returns to inspire and focus our longing to respond to the planet's need and to the urgent spiritual and ecological crisis of our time. The name Gaia gives us someone to imagine and relate to, rather than something to dominate and control, and restores to us the lost feeling of relationship with Earth as

STATUE OF ATHENA c. 520 B.C.

Mother. But Gaia was more than Great Mother as source and foundation of all that is. She was also the active and dynamic consciousness guiding and structuring the ordering of creation. She was the life ensouling it and the law directing it.

The Divine Feminine in Greece stands between two visions, two phases of human evolutionary experience – one focused on the goddess and the other on the god. In Greece the awesome powers of the older Great Mother of the Neolithic and the Bronze Ages were divided among goddesses who carried different aspects of her being. The influence of a patriarchal culture is shown by the fact that Athena, Aphrodite, Artemis, and Persephone are daughters of Zeus by various goddesses and he is now the supreme father of the gods. But Gaia as well as her daughter Demeter bring through into Greek culture the maternal dimension of the older Great Mother who was the life of the Earth and the source of all the gods.

The Homeric hymns to the goddesses are among the finest expressions of the Greek spirit. Through them we can feel the close relationship with the numinous, the love of beauty and harmony that was so profound an expression of the Greek soul. Through the fertile imagery of their ancient words, we hear a hymn of praise to life. A divine presence is invoked, at once transcendent and immanent, godlike and human. The same feminine presence pervades the pages of the *Odyssey* where Penelope is the focus of Odysseus's long quest and Athena his constant and luminous guide.

All the goddesses still transmit the feeling of the earlier time, the feeling that the Divine Feminine could be appealed to for help, guidance, and inspiration. Through their image, people were made aware that they walked on sacred ground, that they lived within a sacred reality where everything they were and everything they experienced was rooted in that ground. As in Egypt, on every side hidden beings were intermediaries between earth and heaven, connecting the dimension of the physical world to the unseen dimension that ensouled it. There was no rigid line drawn between what was imagination and what was reality. The human soul was part of the greater soul of nature that was alive with these unseen beings. The powers and

THE SNAKE GODDESS OF CRETE
John Duncan

qualities of this greater soul were named as goddesses and gods, so people had an image that reflected not only the unseen dimension of life but also the unseen dimension of their own nature. This gave them the possibility of orienting their own lives to this dimension, keeping in touch with it, gaining knowledge of it, and applying this knowledge to the development of their soul and to the creation of an extraordinary civilization.

THE BIRTH OF VENUS
Sandro Botticelli
1445–1510

Athena was the Goddess of Wisdom and the Great Goddess of Greece. Her greatest gift to her people was the olive tree   the Greek Tree of Life – its rich golden oil a symbol of her divine wisdom; its delicious fruit her nourishing food. Although Athena came from the older Bronze Age culture of Crete, in Greece she becomes the inspiration of its astounding artistic and intellectual flowering. She is described in the *Odyssey* as a tall and beautiful woman, with piercing, brilliant eyes, wearing a white robe and a goatskin cloak, the *aegis*, emblazoned with the severed head of the Gorgon. Like Isis, Inanna, and Ishtar before her, Athena is Virgin and yet, like them, she also has the tremendous stature of the Great Mother. In statues and vase paintings she takes two forms. One is a helmeted warrior maiden, the fearsome protectress of her city, Athens. But another, older Athena is reflected in a magnificent statue (c. 525 B.C.) from the archaic temple on the Acropolis, which shows her head crowned with snakes, and her cloak falling from her shoulders as a mass of entwined snakes, with one clasped in her left hand. The snake imagery, signifying her power to regenerate life, shows her descent from the Great Goddess of an earlier age. Often in the *Odyssey*, Athena is described as a swallow or sea-eagle; and these, together with the owl that was often shown with her and was an image of her wisdom, bring Athena close to Bronze Age Crete, Sumer, and Egypt. There the bird was both the messenger of the goddess and her immanent presence, not only guiding the living but also accompanying the dead on their journey to the hidden realms of her being.

Athena was the inspiration of the brilliant flowering of Greek civilization in her city, Athens, where she was patroness of all arts and handicrafts, the heroic embodiment of the intellectual genius of the Greek soul. In the *Odyssey*, Athena personifies wisdom, foresight, and reflective intelligence as she brings Odysseus home to Penelope. In the *Odyssey* as well as in the story of Perseus and Medusa, she teaches her heroes to use the power of reflection to transform the instinctive response to fear (being turned to stone) into resolute, courageous action. Athena embodies the wisdom of the Divine Feminine to guide and instruct humanity, no longer containing her child as the Great Mother did in earlier ages, but helping it to develop the creative gifts and talents bestowed by her.

Artemis, the Moon Goddess, is the descendent of the Neolithic Goddess of the Animals. She is perhaps the most archaic of the Greek goddesses. Her cult with its sacrificial rites and orgiastic, ecstatic dances may have come originally from the great mountains and forests of Anatolia (modern Turkey) and was descended from rituals there many thousands of years old. The extraordinary, black, many-breasted statue of Artemis, adorned with bulls, lions, deer, and winged figures, that once stood in her temple at Ephesus, portrays her as the Great Mother, worshiped for many thousands of years all over Anatolia, where one of her many names was Cybele. In her mythology and her cult, Artemis inherits the inexhaustible power of the Great Goddess to create, destroy, and regenerate life, but this power is not easily recognized in the figure of the young huntress, daughter of Zeus,

STATUE OF ARTEMIS
AT EPHESUS

described in the Homeric hymn to her. Guardian of newborn life in human beings and animals, patroness of midwives, and protectress of mothers in childbirth, Artemis was worshiped in Greece more than any other goddess. She stands at the threshold where life comes into being or expires, in the wild, desolate places, the deep forest, and high mountains, the secret groves, and rushing streams where nature is most felt and feared. Agamemnon sacrificed his daughter Iphigenia to her, in order to secure a fair wind to bring his fleet to Troy. Artemis personifies life as instinct, nature as instinct, its mighty creative, destructive, and transforming power and energy; wild, untameable, premoral. She is close in feeling to Sekhmet in Egypt, Inanna in Sumer, and Kali in India. There is cruelty, even savagery in Artemis (and in those who sacrificed to her): the animals who were once her life are afraid of her hunting cry and her sharp, unerring arrows. Hundreds were sacrificed at night to her in her temples in much the same way as they are sacrificed to this day in India to Kali. Yet Artemis was also the protectress of life, and she, of all the Greek goddesses, would have been invoked to protect nature from the desecration inflicted on her by mortals.

Aphrodite, born from the sea foam, is Goddess of Love, Desire, and Beauty. She is not a gentle goddess but the mighty power of instinct that can move the human heart to the heights of ecstasy or the depths of despair. The Greeks knew Aphrodite as the inspiration of their joy and sensuous delight in life, who overwhelmed them with powerful feelings of attraction for another human being, with the ecstatic passion of love, or the terror of loss and abandonment. The incarnation of beauty, the goddess was adorned with the flowers and jewels that were the most exquisite expression of life's impulse to create. Aphrodite was the body's happiness at being alive, its experience of belonging to a greater whole. Like Hathor in Egypt, she personified the boundless fecundity of life, the creative energy that acts as the sexual impulse in animals and human beings, the uprush of vitality and fertility in the spring, the flowering of the earth in its miraculous beauty. For the Greeks, Aphrodite was their love of beauty and their response to beauty in all forms. Poetry, art, and music were her mode of expression. Whatever delighted and entranced the eye, the ear, the touch, and the senses in general, these were the gift of Aphrodite and were therefore sacred to her.

Christianity was afraid of the goddess and banished Aphrodite, seeing her as the embodiment of everything it feared in Eve and all women who embodied her beauty. Delight in the body, sensuality, and sexual desire were all associated with temptation and sin and were therefore condemned. Aphrodite's gifts of beauty, delight, and ecstasy were repudiated. But if Aphrodite is not allowed to live in us, the soul falls into depression and despair. The greatest sickness in Christian culture has been the fear

THE BIRTH OF VENUS *Odilon Redon* 1840–1916

and desacralization of sexuality, the denigration and denial of the ecstatic, the repression of delight in life, and the devaluation and fear of women. The body in particular has suffered from being feared and despised. This repression of instinct has led in this century to the tremendous reaction against all forms of authority and the swing to sexual excess without, unfortunately, understanding why this has happened and recovering the sacred dimension of sexuality. Where Aphrodite is not honored she returns in negative form as the sexual compulsions, pornography, and sadistic fantasies that have taken possession of our culture.

The myth of Demeter and Persephone is the most dramatically alive of all Greek myths, as relevant and moving for us today as it was for generations of Greeks long ago. Recited or sung yearly at the great festival of the Thesmophoria in the temple at Eleusis, it must have put all who listened to it in touch with their deepest feelings of grief and hope. Egypt had an immense influence on Greece, and beneath the Greek lunar myth of Demeter's search for her daughter Persephone is the Egyptian myth of Isis's search for Osiris and Ishtar's search for her son Tammuz, lost in the underworld. In all three there is the same timeless theme of loss, quest, reunion, and the return of life after death. From the Greek myth came the Mysteries of Eleusis, which were celebrated there for more than a thousand years. To those who were initiated into the vision of the Mysteries, these gave a deep sense of happiness and hope, trust in the survival of the soul and the reunion with loved ones after death. They were one of the most powerful and ancient rituals ever devised for keeping alive the sense of relationship with the Divine Feminine as the eternal ground of life. Much later, in the Gnostic myth of Sophia, the same theme of the separation and reunion of the Mother and the Daughter reappears as a story of the soul's separation from, and reunion with, the divine ground of its origin.

The Homeric hymn to Demeter tells the story of the abduction of Persephone, daughter of Demeter and Zeus, into the underworld realm of Hades, Lord of the Kingdom of the Dead. The myth is a story of loss and recovery, of death and rebirth, and was perhaps the surviving ritual of an earlier age when agricultural peoples mourned the death of the crops in the winter and celebrated the renewal of life in the spring. Demeter is the Great Mother of Life. Her grief reflects maternal anguish, but not maternal powerlessness. Awesome, majestic, personifying the Law of Life to which even the gods are subject, she throws Mount Olympos into disarray, plunging the earth into drought because of her rage and grief. Zeus is forced to yield to her longing to be reunited with her daughter.

Many of Zeus's amorous exploits were described in terms of rape, and the story of Persephone's rape by Hades follows this pattern. Seen from another perspective, however, Persephone's rape describes the feminine initiation into sexuality and the separation of a daughter from her mother. It may also be understood as a shamanic initiation into a deeper dimension of reality beyond the outer forms of nature.

Persephone is the only goddess who moves, like Inanna in Sumer, between the bright solar world and the dark lunar underworld of life, thereby keeping them in touch with each other. Her initiation into the realm of the mysteries comes as a rape into the unseen depths of life from which she emerges no longer a young, innocent girl but Queen of the Underworld, a mature woman, and a mother, bringing new life with her in the form of her son, fruit of her union with Hades.

The Homeric hymn reveals the uneasy marriage between a new sky god culture and an older goddess one. In the "takeover" by Zeus, Hades, and Poseidon of the dimensions of heaven, the underworld, and the sea, and the attempted imposition of Zeus's will on Demeter and Persephone, we can sense the cultural change of consciousness as the Great Goddess, who once included these three realms in her being, loses her former position to Zeus and his brothers. But this change of emphasis can be understood to reflect a new phase in the evolution of human consciousness, one where the developing power of mind and rational thought, personified by the image of the god, begins to draw away from the maternal realm of nature and soul in order to know itself and the universe and to discover its origin and destiny. The dangers of losing touch altogether with the Divine Feminine are visible today in the spiritual and ecological crisis that is such an immense challenge to us, yet in becoming aware of what has been lost, we can find ways to heal the dissociation between mind and soul.

THE HOMERIC
HYMN TO ARTEMIS

*Artemis I sing, with her golden arrows
and her hunting cry, the sacred maiden
deer-huntress, showering arrows,
sister of Apollo with his golden sword.*

*In mountains of shadow and peaks of wind
she delights in the chase, she arches her bow
of solid gold, she lets fly arrows that moan.*

*Crests of high mountains tremble,
the forest in darkness screams
with the terrible howling of wild animals.
The earth itself shudders,
even the sea alive with fish.*

*But the heart of the goddess is strong,
she darts everywhere
in and out, every way,
killing the race of beasts.*

*And when she has had enough of looking
     for animals,
this huntress who takes pleasure in arrows,
when her heart is elated, then she unstrings
her curved bow and goes
to the great house of Phoebus Apollo,
her dear brother,
in the fertile grasslands of Delphi.*

*And there she arranges
the lovely dance of the Muses and Graces.*

*There she hangs up her unstrung bow
and her quiver of arrows,
and gracefully clothing her body
she takes first place at the dances
     and begins.*

*With heavenly voices they all sing.
They sing of Leto with her lovely ankles,
how she gave birth to the best children
of all the gods, supreme
in what they say and do.*

*Farewell, children of Zeus and Leto,
she of the beautiful hair.
Now, and in another song
I will remember you.*

FROM *The Myth of the Goddess*
BY ANNE BARING AND JULES CASHFORD
TRANSLATED BY JULES CASHFORD

THE HOMERIC HYMN TO ATHENA

PALLAS Athena I shall sing,
The glorious goddess
   whose eyes gleam,
brilliantly inventive,
   her heart relentless,
formidable maiden,
   guardian of cities,
the courageous Tritogeneia.

Wise Zeus gave birth to
   her himself
   out of his majestic head.
Golden armor clothed her,
   it was glistening, warlike.
All the gods who saw her
   were overcome with awe

Suddenly she was there,
   before Zeus who holds the aegis.
She sprang from his immortal head,
   shaking her sharp spear.

Great Olympos trembled terribly
   at the power of the goddess
   with the gleaming eyes.
And all around her the earth
   screamed awfully and then the sea
started to move,
   frothing with dark waves,

and salt foam suddenly spurted up.
The brilliant son of Hyperion, the sun,
   stilled his swift-footed horses
   for a long time until
Pallas Athena, the maiden,
   unclasped the godlike (heavenly)
   armor
from her immortal shoulders.
   Wise Zeus was delighted.

Greetings, daughter of Zeus who
   holds the aegis.
Now, and in another song,
   I will remember you.

FROM *The Myth of the Goddess*
BY ANNE BARING AND JULES CASHFORD
TRANSLATED BY JULES CASHFORD

THE HOMERIC HYMNS TO APHRODITE

Golden crowned, beautiful awesome
Aphrodite is who I shall sing,
she who possesses the heights of
all sea-wet Cyprus where Zephyros
swept her with his moist breath over the
waves of the roaring sea in soft foam.

In their circles of gold the Hours joyously
received her and wrapped the ambrosial
garments around her.

On her immortal head they laid a crown
of gold that was wonderfully made and
in the pierced lobes of her ears they hung
flowers of copper from the mountains
and precious gold.

Round her delicate throat and her silvery
breasts they fastened necklaces of gold which
they, the gold-filleted Hours wear themselves
when they go to the lovely dances of the
gods in their father's house.

And when they had arranged
all those decorations on her body
then they led her to the immortal gods
who saw her and welcomed her and reached
out their hands toward her

Longing, every one of them, to take her
home to be his lawful wife, so enraptured
were they all with the beauty of the
Cytherean crowned in violets.

Farewell quick-glancing
sweet-smiling goddess.
Grant me victory in this contest,
favor my song.

And now and in another song
I shall remember you.

FROM *The Myth of the Goddess*
BY ANNE BARING AND JULES CASHFORD
TRANSLATED BY JULES CASHFORD

THE BIRTH OF VENUS, FROM THE LUDOVISI THRONE
c. 470–460 B.C.

THE HOMERIC HYMN
TO DEMETER

Demeter, thick-haired Demeter,
*   sacred goddess,*
I shall sing, of her and her daughter
with the slender ankles whom
*   Aidoneus seized away*
and loud-thundering, far-seeing Zeus
*   gave her away*
far from Demeter with her
*   golden sword*
and her glorious harvests, the
*   daughter was playing*
with the deep-breasted daughters
*   of Oceanus.*
They were gathering flowers, roses and
*   crocuses*
and beautiful violets in a soft meadow,
there were irises and hyacinths and a narcissus
which Gaia grew as a snare for the
*   flower-like girl,*
for Zeus willed it and The Receiver of Many
wanted it, and the flower shone
*   wondrously.*

Everyone who saw it was amazed,
*   immortal gods*
as well as mortal men. From its root
*   there grew*
a hundred blooms which had a scent
*   so sweet that all*
the wide heaven above and all the
*   earth and all*
the salt swelling of the sea laughed aloud.
And the girl too wondered at it,
*   she reached out*
her hands to take this thing
*   of such delight,*
but the earth with wide paths gaped in
*   the plain of Nysa,*
and the Lord, The Receiver of Many,
*   sprang upon her*
with his immortal horses, that son of
*   Cronos with many names.*

He caught hold of her, protesting, and he
*   took her away,*
weeping, in his chariot of gold.
Then she screamed in a shrill voice,
*   calling for her father,*

the almighty and invincible Son of Cronos.
But no one, neither the immortal gods
   nor mortal men,
no one heard her voice, not even the
   olive trees
heavy with fruit...

Yet the goddess, as long as she could
   see the earth
and the sparkling sky and the
   fast-flowing sea
full of fishes and the light of the sun,
and as long as she still hoped to look upon
her dear mother and the race of gods
   who live forever,
then that hope charmed her great heart

in spite of her grief...
And the peaks of the mountains and the
   depths of the sea echoed
with her immortal voice, and her queenly
   mother heard her.
A sharp pain seized her heart. With her
   lovely hands
she tore the veil from her long
   ambrosial hair,
she let fall her dark blue cloak from
   off her shoulders
and like a solitary wild bird
   she streaked out
across dry land and sea, searching...

FROM *The Myth of the Goddess*
BY ANNE BARING AND JULES CASHFORD
TRANSLATED BY JULES CASHFORD

DEMETER AND PERSEPHONE WITH TRIPTOLEMOS C.440 B.C.

CHAPTER SEVEN

THE SHEKINAH OF JUDAISM

Beloved and Bride

I am the Rose of Sharon and the Lily of the Valleys.

*T*he Shekinah is the image of the Divine Feminine or the feminine face of God as it was conceived in the mystical tradition of Judaism, originating perhaps in the rabbinic schools of Babylon and transmitted orally for a thousand years until it flowered in the writings of the Jewish Kabbalists of medieval Spain and southwestern France. In Kabbalah, religion ceases to be a matter of worship and collective belief. It becomes a direct path of communion between the individual and the Divine. In the imagery of the Shekinah, Kabbalah gives us the cosmology of the soul and the relationship between the two aspects of the godhead that has been lost or hidden for millennia. The mythology of Kabbalah is so gloriously rich, so broad in its imaginative and revelatory reach, and so intensely nourishing to a world that lacks any awareness of the Divine Feminine, that to discover this tradition is immensely exciting. The Shekinah reveals the missing imagery of God-as-Mother that has been lost or obscured in both Judaism and Christianity.

Whereas the Old Testament is the written tradition of Judaism, Kabbalah offers the hidden oral tradition, wonderfully named as "The Voice of the Turtle" (turtledove). This mystic knowledge or mystic tradition of the direct path to God was described as the Jewels of the Heavenly Bride. The Bronze Age imagery of the Great Goddess returns to life in the extraordinary beauty of the Kabbalistic descriptions of the Shekinah and in the gender endings of nouns that describe the feminine dimension of the godhead. But the Divine Feminine is now understood as cosmic soul, the intermediary between the godhead and life in this dimension who, as the Shekinah, brings together heaven and earth, the divine and the human in a resplendent vision of their essential relationship.

The mythology of this tradition restores the image of the sacred marriage in the union of the Divine Father-Mother in the ground of being. There is not a Mother and a Father but the Mother-Father who are one in their eternal embrace: one in their ground, one in their emanation, one in their ecstatic and continuous act of creation through all the invisible dimensions they bring into being and sustain. No other tradition offers the same breathtaking vision, in such exquisite poetic imagery, of the union of male and female energies in the One that is both. The Song of Songs was the text most used by Kabbalists for their contemplation of the mystery of this divine union. Yet one has the feeling that this way to union with the Divine may descend from some unknown source that nourished Egypt, Sumer, and India.

The Kabbalistic tradition describes the feminine image of the godhead as Mother, Daughter, Sister, and Holy Spirit, giving woman what she has lacked throughout the last two and a half thousand years in Judeo-Christian culture — an image of the Divine Feminine in the godhead that is reflected at the human level in herself. The Shekinah is Divine Motherhood, Mother of All Living. Women can know themselves, in their role as mothers, in their care and concern for the well-being of their loved ones, as the instinctive custodians of her creation.

The thirteenth-century *Zohar, The Book of Radiance or Splendor* that was the principal text of Kabbalah, contemplates the mystery of the relationship between the female and male aspects of the godhead expressed as Mother and Father, and their emanation through all levels of creation as Daughter and Son. The essential conception of this mystical tradition expresses itself as an image of worlds within worlds. Divine Spirit (*Ain Soph* or *Ein Sof*) beyond form or conception is the light at the center, the heart, and moves outward as creative sound (word), thought, and energy, bringing into being successive spheres, realms, veils, or dimensions imagined as veils or robes that clothe and hide the hidden source yet at the same time transmit its radiant light.

The transmission of light from source to the outer, manifest level is also imagined as an inverted tree, the Tree of Life, whose branches grow from its root in the divine ground and extend through the worlds of emanation. The primal center or root is the innermost light, of an unimaginable luminosity and translucence. The inner point expands or is sown as a ray of light into a dimension described in some texts as a sea of glory, in others as a palace that acts as an enclosure for the light; from this womb it emanates as a radiant cascade, a fountain of living water, pouring forth light to sustain and permeate all the worlds or dimensions it brings into being. All life on earth, all consciousness, is that light and is therefore utterly sacred. The *Zohar* describes nature as the garment of God.

The Shekinah or feminine face of the godhead is the Cosmic Womb, the Palace, the Enclosure, the Fountain, Apple Orchard, and Mystical Garden of Eden and, at the same time, the radiance that becomes the successive robes or veils that are the spheres of consciousness or dimensions of created life. She is named as Mother, Sister, and Daughter, Beloved and Bride, the architect of worlds, the source or foundation of our world, who is the Radiance, Word, or Glory of the unknowable ground or godhead; she brings into being all the creative powers and entities, both female and male (the ten *sephiroth*), all the spheres or dimensions of manifestation that are ensouled by the godhead until she generates the manifest world we know.

The Kabbalists called this last sphere Malkuth, the Kingdom, where the divine Mother-Father image is expressed as the male and female of all species. Humanity, female and male, is made in the image of God, the reflection of the duality-in-unity of the godhead. The Shekinah is forever united with her beloved spouse in the divine ground or heart of being, and it is their union in the godhead that holds life in a constant state of coming into being. The sexual attraction between man and woman and the expression of true love between them is the enactment or reflection at this level of creation of the divine embrace at its heart enshrined in the words: "I am my Beloved's and my Beloved is mine." Human sexual relationship, enacted with love, mutual respect, and joy, is a holy ritual that helps to maintain the ecstatic union of the divine pair.

Text after text uses sexual imagery and the imagery of light to describe how the ray that emerges from nothing is sown into the womb – the Great Sea of Light – of the celestial Mother and how she brings forth from this womb the male and female creative energies, which, as two branches of the Tree of Life, are King and Queen, Son and Daughter. A third branch of the Tree descends directly down the center, unifying the energies on either side. Surely a long visionary tradition, meditated on for centuries, must lie behind these images. The Shekinah is the waters above and below the firmament, the Divine Spouse, the indwelling and active Holy Spirit, and the divine guide or immanent presence who delivers the world from bondage and restores it ultimately to the heavenly spheres. Wisdom, compassion, justice, and mercy are four intrinsic qualities of her being; yet, like the goddesses of Egypt and Sumer, she can also be terrible in her power to destroy and in her fury at the wanton desecration of her life.

Because she brings all worlds into existence as her robes or veils, and dwells in them as Divine Presence, nothing is outside God, nothing excluded. Everything is connected to everything else as through a luminous circulatory system, a seamless robe of light. Moreover, the Shekinah is deeply devoted to what she has brought into

ADAM AND EVE *Lucas Cranach the Elder* 1472–1553

THE LITTLE PARADISE GARDEN
The Master of the Paradise Garden
c. 1410

being, as a mother is devoted to the well-being of her child and, in particular, to the mystic community of Israel.

In the last chapter of the Book of Revelation (Rev. 21:2), written by a Jewish Christian hand, the imagery of the Shekinah can be recognized in the description of the Heavenly City, "descending from heaven, prepared as a bride adorned for her husband" with pearls and gold and precious jewels, having no need of sun or moon for light, for she is the Light, the Glory of God. Christians, knowing nothing of this lost tradition, cannot make the connection between the Shekinah as Bride and the Holy Spirit, the feminine aspect of the divine.

There were different schools of Kabbalah. Some saw the Shekinah as separated from the godhead, in voluntary exile on earth, describing her as a daughter cut off from her mother, and as a widow, until she is able to return to the divine ground, having gathered to herself all the elements or sparks of her light that had been scattered throughout creation during the process of emanation. The blackness of the Shekinah's robe, inherited perhaps from the black robe or veil of Isis (who was also called "The Widow" during her search for Osiris), is the darkness of the mystery that hides the hidden glory of her Light.

Another strand in this tapestry of the Divine Feminine in the Hebrew tradition are the Wisdom Books of the Old Testament (of which the greater part were mysteriously lost), written down from the fourth to the first centuries B.C., after the end of the Captivity in Babylon. The Shekinah comes to life in the passages where Wisdom (called Hokhmah in Hebrew, or Sophia in Greek) speaks as the Holy Spirit calling to humanity. She tells us that she is immanent in our world, with us in the streets of our cities, calling to us to awaken to her presence, to obey her laws, to listen to her wisdom, promising her blessing if we can only hear her voice and respond to her teaching. These magnificent passages transform the voice of the Shekinah, speaking as Divine Wisdom, from abstract idea into presence, friend, and guide. She speaks as if she were here, in this dimension, dwelling in the midst of her kingdom, accessible to those who seek her out. Widowed because of her voluntary separation from her spouse, she is unknown and unrecognized, yet working within the depths of life, striving to open humanity's understanding to her justice, her wisdom, and her truth.

She says that she is with her beloved from the beginning, before the foundation of the world, speaking from the deep ground of life as the hidden law that orders it, the craftswoman of creation. She is the intelligence within nature, the animating energy of the cosmos; rooted in tree, vine, earth, and water and active in the habitations of humanity. She is the principle of justice that inspires all human laws. She is the invisible spirit guiding human consciousness; a hidden presence longing to be known, calling out to the world for recognition and response. To those like Solomon, who prized her more highly than rubies, she becomes their wise and luminous guide.

Yet another strand to this story is the Gnostic imagery of the Divine Mother Sophia. Reading the Kabbalistic texts, it is almost as if they are the voice of this lost tradition. By the year 200, all the feminine imagery of God that was part of the Gnostic tradition had been excised from the orthodox canon of Christian teaching so that, until very recently in this century, no one knew that some groups of early Christians had an image of the Divine Mother. They named her the "Invisible within the All." They spoke of how, as the Eternal Silence, she received the seed of light from the ineffable source and how, from this womb, she brought forth all the emanations of light, ranged in harmonious pairs of feminine and masculine energies. They saw her as the womb of life, not only of human life, but the life of the whole cosmos. They named this Divine Mother as Holy Spirit and saw the dove as her emissary: at the baptism of Jesus, it was the Divine Mother who spoke to her son.

The imagery and mythology of the Divine Mother in Gnosticism is so similar to her later imagery as the Shekinah of Kabbalah that they seem to belong to one and the same tradition. In a Gnostic text called the *Trimorphic Protennoia*, the speaker describes herself as the intangible Womb that gives shape to the All, the life that moves in every creature. Other texts name her as the Mother of the Universe but also speak of the androgyny of the divine source in imagery similar to the later Kabbalistic texts.

Today we might imagine the Shekinah as the light that manifests as both wave and particle, as the deep unexplored "sea" of cosmic space, and as the extraordinary complex structure and organization of energy manifested as matter – a word that comes from the Latin word for mother: *mater*. After so many billions of years the energy of life has evolved a form – the planet earth – and a consciousness – our own – which is slowly helping us to explore the mystery of what we are. Yet, because of the loss of the tradition of the Divine Feminine, we do not know that what we are exploring in the finer and finer gradations of matter we discover is what the Jewish mystics called the face and the glory of God, nor that the universe we explore with

THE   SHEKINAH   OF   JUDAISM :   BELOVED   &   BRIDE

our technology is the outer covering or veil of an unimaginable web of luminous interconnecting pathways. If only these images of the Shekinah could be restored to us, how differently we might see matter, with what respect and awe we might treat it.

In the magnificent passages from the Apocrypha, it seems as if the Shekinah is telling us her story:

I came out of the mouth of the most high,
*   and covered the earth as a cloud.*
I dwelt in high places,
*   and my throne is in a cloudy pillar.*
I alone compassed the circuit of heaven,
*   and walked in the bottom of the deep.*
I had power over the waves of the sea,
*   and over all the earth,*
and over every people and nation...

He created me from the beginning
*   before the world, and I shall never fail.*
In the holy tabernacle I served before him;
*   and so was I established in Sion.*

Likewise in the beloved city he gave me rest,
*   and in Jerusalem was my power...*

I am the mother of fair love, and fear,
*   and knowledge and holy hope...*
I therefore, being eternal, am given to
*   all my children which are named of him.*
Come unto me, all ye that be desirous of me,
*   and fill yourselves with my fruits.*
For my memorial is sweeter than honey,
*   and mine inheritance than the honey-*
*   comb...*

WISDOM OF JESUS BEN SIRACH
24:3–6, 9–11, 18–20

I also came out as a brook
   from a river,
and as a conduit into a garden.
I said, I will water my best garden,
and will water abundantly my
   garden bed:
and lo, my brook became a river,
and my river became a sea.
I will yet make doctrine to
   shine as the morning,
and will send forth her light
   afar off.
I will yet pour out doctrine
   as prophecy,
and leave it to all ages for ever.
Behold that I have not labored for
   myself only,
but for all them that seek wisdom.

WISDOM OF JESUS BEN SIRACH
24:30–4

WHO can number the sand
   of the sea,
And the drops of rain,
And the days of eternity?
Who can find out the height
   of heaven,
And the breadth of the earth,
And the deep, and Wisdom?
Wisdom hath been created before
   all things,
And the understanding of prudence
   from everlasting.
The word of God most high
   is the fountain of Wisdom;
And her ways are everlasting
   commandments.
To whom hath the root of Wisdom
   been revealed?
Or who hath known her
   wise counsels?

WISDOM OF JESUS BEN SIRACH 1: 2–6

As a mother shall she meet him...
With the Bread of Understanding
   shall she feed him,
And give him the Water of Wisdom
   to drink.

WISDOM OF JESUS BEN SIRACH 15:2–3

I WAS sent forth from the power
and I have come to those who reflect
   upon me,
and I have been found among those
   who seek after me.
Look upon me, you who reflect
   upon me,
and you hearers, hear me...

For I am the First and the Last,
I am the honored one and the
   scorned one,
I am the Whore and the Holy One.
I am the Wife and the Virgin.
I am the Mother and the Daughter.
I am the members of my mother.
I am the barren one and many
   are her sons.

I am the Silence that is
   incomprehensible
and the idea whose remembrance is
   frequent.
I am the Voice whose Sound is
   manifold
and the Word whose appearance
   is multiple
I am the utterance of my Name...

I am knowledge and ignorance...
I am strength and I am fear.
I am war and peace.
Give heed to me...

Hear me, you hearers, and learn of
my words, you who know me.
I am the Hearing that is attainable
   to everything;
I am the Speech that cannot
   be grasped.
I am the name of the Sound
and the Sound of the Name...

I am the One who alone exists,
and I have no one who will judge me.

FROM THE THUNDER, PERFECT MIND
The Nag Hammadi Library
TRANSLATED BY G.W. MACRAE

*W*isdom is glorious, and
   never fadeth away:
yea, she is easily seen of them
   that love her,
and found of such as seek her.
She preventeth them that desire her,
in making herself first known
   unto them.
Whoso seeketh her early shall have
   no great travail,
for he shall find her sitting at his doors.
To think therefore upon her is
   perfection of wisdom,
and whoso watcheth for her shall
   quickly be without care.

WISDOM OF SOLOMON 6:12–15

I AM Protennoia,
The Thought that dwells in the Light.
I am the movement that dwells
    in the All,
She who exists before the All,
She in whom the All takes its stand.
I am Invisible within the Thought of
    the Invisible One.
I am revealed in the immeasurable,
    ineffable things.
I am intangible, dwelling in
    the intangible.
I move in every creature...
and those who sleep I awaken.

I am the Invisible One within the All.
I am the immeasurable, ineffable, yet
    whenever I wish,
I shall reveal myself.
I am the movement of the All.
I exist before the All, and I am the All,
Since I exist before everyone.

I am a Voice speaking softly.
I exist from the first.
I dwell within the Silence...
And it is the hidden Voice that dwells
    within me,
Within the intangible,
    immeasurable Thought

Within the immeasurable Silence.
I descended to the midst of the
    underworld
And I shone down upon the darkness.
It is I who poured forth the Water.
I am the one hidden within
    Radiant Waters.
I am the one who gradually dawns on
    the All...

I am the Image of the Invisible
    Spirit...
I am the Womb that gives shape
    to the All.
By giving birth to the Light that shines
    in splendor.

FROM THE TRIMORPHIC PROTENNOIA
The Nag Hammadi Library
TRANSLATED BY J.D. TURNER

*I prayed and understanding was
given me: I called upon God, and the Spirit
of Wisdom came to me...
I loved her above health and beauty, and
chose to have her instead of light, for the
light that cometh from her never goeth out...*

*And all such things as are either secret or
manifest, them I know.
For Wisdom, which is the worker of all
things, taught me; for in her is an
understanding spirit, holy, one only,
manifold, subtil, lively, clear, undefiled, plain,
not subject to hurt, loving the thing that is
good, quick, which cannot be letted, ready to
do good, kind to man, stedfast, sure, free
from care, having all power, overseeing all
things, and going through all understanding,
pure, and most subtil, spirits.*

*For Wisdom is more moving than any
motion: she passeth and goeth through all
things by reason of her pureness.*

*For she is the breath of the power of God,
and a pure influence flowing from the glory
of the Almighty: therefore can no defiled
thing fall into her.
For she is the brightness of the everlasting
Light, the unspotted mirror of the power of
God, and the image of his goodness...*

*She is more beautiful than the sun, and
above all the order of stars: being compared
with the Light, she is found before it...*

*Wisdom reacheth from one end to another
mightily: and sweetly doth she order all
things. I loved her, and sought her out
from my youth, I desired to make her my
spouse, and I was a lover of her beauty.*

WISDOM OF SOLOMON 7:7, 10, 21–7, 29; 8:1–2

CHAPTER EIGHT

QUEEN OF HEAVEN

Christianity

Hail! Queen of Heaven,
Hail! Lady of the Angels:
Salutation to Thee, root and portal,
Whence the Light of the world has arisen.

Those who know only the Christian tradition do not know how deep the roots of Mary go or how the prayers to her echo the immemorial prayers to ancient goddesses. The words above echo the greeting addressed four thousand years ago to the goddesses Inanna, Ishtar, and Isis as Queen of Heaven – Hail! Great Lady of Heaven! Hail! Light of the World! Mary, like these older goddesses, is personified by the morning star as well as by the moon, whose crescent is often shown beneath her feet. Like Isis, Mary became the Queen of the Sea, guardian of the waters, and, like Artemis and Aphrodite in Greece, and Kuan Yin in China and Japan, she presides over fertility and childbirth. Millions of people, particularly women, have prayed to Mary as they once did to Ishtar, Hathor, Isis, and Kuan Yin, giving thanks to her for safe delivery in childbirth and leaving countless tokens of gratitude in her shrines for answers to their appeals for her help in the crises of their lives.

CORONATION OF THE VIRGIN *Moulin Master* fl. 1480–1500

Although Mary is appealed to as Queen of Heaven, she seems to stand, as intercessor between earth and heaven, for the connecting principle of life, for the soul – for the feminine principle of relationship that connects all things to each other, for the supreme values of the heart. She is the grail of compassion and healing. She is the guardian of the sacredness of all life. When the Virgin Mary appears in visions, as at Fatima and Medjugorje, it is to children that she speaks. She speaks as if she were the voice of the Holy Spirit, offering wisdom and warning, and the children who see her and hear her voice, knowing nothing of what they ought or ought not to believe, respond instinctively from the soul, implicitly trusting what she is saying to them. In these messages, she does not ask for belief but for radical and total transformation.

The full dimensions of the Virgin Mary are more easily understood if we look beyond her to the luminous image of the Shekinah. In the Shekinah we are one life, one radiance. So many numinous images that belonged to the Shekinah in the Old Testament were transferred to Mary; reflection on Mary as intercessor between God and humanity reveals the veiled form of the Shekinah as the feminine face of God, the divine presence within all created life. Perhaps we may recognize her in Mary's mother, St. Anne. The painters of the Renaissance show Mary's womb penetrated by a ray of light from God in the way that the ray or point of light from the source penetrated the "sea of glory" of the Shekinah's womb.

Mary's name is derived from the Latin *mare* – the sea – one of the most ancient images of the waters of life, the great sea of being. Mary gradually reveals herself to be the Prima Materia, the Root and Portal of Life, the Womb of Creation, the Fountain, and the Rose Garden – images that also belonged to the Shekinah. Like the Shekinah, she is the secret, hidden ground of the soul, addressed as such by many Christian mystics, the conduit to the Divine. Many of the images evoked in the great Orthodox Akathist hymn to Mary address her as this ineffable ground: the height unattainable by human thought; the depth invisible even to the eyes of angels; the womb of divine incarnation; the field of the immortal crop; the planter of our life; the haven; the fount of love; the inexhaustible treasure. Mary is the rose, the lily, and the Tree of Life from which the faithful are fed – an image that evokes not only the Shekinah as the image of the hidden wisdom that is the Tree of Life but also the goddesses Nut, Hathor, and Isis giving the food and drink of eternal life to the souls of the dead.

Wherever the association is made between love and divinity, between beauty and harmony and divinity, between nourishment and divinity, or between compassion and divinity, there stands the image of the Divine Feminine. All of these images, read as describing the unfathomable ground of being that is also the unfathomable ground of the human soul, bring Mary closer to us as the root and foundation of our own lives. She feels closer to us than the transcendent God who has been drawn more in the imagery of a remote father and stern judge than a loving mother. The Virgin Mary is the compassionate, accessible face of the Divine Feminine.

Mary makes few appearances in the Gospels, where she plays a humble and self-effacing role in relation to her son, yet within five hundred years of her death, she has assumed the presence and the stature of all the great goddesses before her. Like them she is both Virgin and Mother. In being named "Mother of God" at the Council of Ephesus in 431, she was implicitly (though not doctrinally) recognized as the feminine counterpart of the Divine Father. The extraordinary story of the elevation of Mary to the stature of Divine Mother shows the immense need of people to have the feminine principle at the heart of their religion, for, as in Egypt and China, it was in response to the appeal of the people that the feminine image of the divine was given or was restored to its former position as Mother of all life.

In her humanity, in her human suffering as the mother of Jesus, Mary brings the divine world closer to human experience, closer to human longing and human suffering. Only Demeter in the Greek world is as human as Mary. As all the Great Mothers did before her, Mary embodies the principle of relationship, the relatedness of the whole of creation to every aspect of itself and to the divine ground that enfolds it. As the Divine Mother, she speaks for the values of the heart, the values that spring from the deepest instincts and feelings in all humanity. So Mary is, in the Christian experience of her, the most intimate and human of Mothers, as the offerings to her in thousands of shrines bear witness. Mary's suffering as a human woman who has given birth to a son, seen him grow to maturity, and lived through the terrible experience of seeing his life sacrificed to human cruelty makes her the sharer of the suffering of all women who have been through the same agonizing experience. Mary's experience makes human suffering bearable because she, as intercessor, is present with it. But if we look at the Christian myth in a deeper sense, we can understand that as the Divine Mother, Mary endures the suffering of the whole of humanity, her "child," until at last we return "home" to her in the divine spheres.

The great Romanesque and Gothic cathedrals that were raised in Mary's honor were imagined as vessels carrying human souls to the safe haven of her harbor. The nave was at once the upturned hull of a ship and (in the Gothic cathedrals) a forest glade where the interlacing branches of the trees met overhead. These images kept

MARY ON A BED OF CORN (detail)
The Rohan Master
c. 1400

alive the ancient connection between the goddess and the sea, and the goddess and the sacred grove of trees that, in older cultures, used to mark her sanctuaries. In these cathedrals stood the magnificent wooden statues of the Virgin in Majesty and the Black Virgins. The finest examples of these were carved in the Auvergne from the eleventh century and show Mary as Theotokos or "Mother of God." They follow the ancient Egyptian statues of Isis as the "Throne" holding her son Horus-Pharaoh on her lap, and show Mary as the Throne of Wisdom with the infant Christ on her lap. He often holds a book, transmitting His blessing and His teaching to the world. Interestingly, the earliest of these statues dates to before the Council of Ephesus in 431 when Mary was officially declared "Mother of God."

Later, the emphasis on Mary as the Throne of Wisdom moves to the image of Mary as the mother of the infant Jesus and closer to the human experience of motherhood. But the numinous, hieratic quality of the older image is retained in the statues of the Black Madonna, which hold their fascination and their healing power to this day. These images are the principal inheritors of the older goddesses, in particular Isis, who was worshiped all over the Roman Empire and whose temples were rededicated to Mary with the coming of Christianity. The color black returns us to the Shulamite – black but beautiful – of the Song of Songs, to the lustrous black robe of Isis, to the widowed Shekinah in exile on earth, whose black veil hides her radiant glory, and to the mystery of life's unfathomable wisdom.

Whereas, in Christian belief, the Virgin Mary is the Mother of God as incarnated in Christ, the older goddesses were the Mother of Life. They were the divine ground manifest as the life of the whole of creation. The Black Virgin reflects the same total vision. But although the cult of the Black Virgin is intrinsically linked to the cult of Mary as the Seat of Wisdom, there is a contradiction implicit in the two images. In Christian culture, the fear of instinct and the belief in original sin have progressively split off nature from spirit. Because of this the image of Mary lacks the deeper dimension of instinct that belongs to the older goddesses. Instinct is placed "beyond

MADONNA OF THE ROSE BOWER *Martin Schöngauer* 1440–1491

THE CORONATION OF THE VIRGIN *Agnolo Gaddi* c. 1370

the pale," associated with the sin of Eve. Mary's own Immaculate Conception and the Virgin Birth of her son place her outside nature. She is below heaven and above nature. This is, perhaps, Christianity's greatest problem: how to include nature and everything pertaining to it in the realm of the Divine, how to recognize the immanence as well as the transcendence of the Divine. The idea that wisdom, once intrinsic to the goddess as the Mother of Life, comes from within nature, and is intrinsic to the life process itself, which is itself within the totality of God, is not easily experienced in relation to Mary except perhaps when we stand in the presence of those masterpieces created by medieval craftsmen and respond to the profound mystery they communicate.

Mary stands at the heart of Christian mystical experience, as did Demeter in Greece and Isis in Egypt, and the Shekinah in the Jewish mystical tradition. She is the mystery sought or stumbled upon in rapture by those who have opened their hearts to the transforming power of her love. Some of the greatest of the Christian mystics, St. Bernard of Clairvaux, Meister Eckhart, St. Thomas Aquinas, St. John of the Cross, have all penetrated to this secret heart of the Christian vision. And they have experienced Mary as the mystical core of their being in the image of their own soul awakening to the hidden revelation it carries. As Angelus Silesius wrote, "I must become Mary and give birth to God." Meister Eckhart spoke often of the greatest Christian mystery – the birthing of Christ within the soul.

The image of the sacred marriage, implicit in the beautiful portrayals of the Coronation of the Virgin Mary by her Son, Christ, reunites the long estranged aspects of the godhead. They sit side by side, united by the same starry robe, each glorifying the other. The image given is of a marriage between the Virgin Mary and Christ who, by his gesture of crowning her, welcomes her as Queen of Heaven and his bride. In these glorified beings, woman and man are shown as the mystery they are and as the enlightened beings they could become. In earlier cultures, such an image would have signified the sacred marriage between sun and moon or between heaven and earth, goddess and god. This sacred marriage is between the two aspects of the Divine, the Queen and King of Heaven. The exiled Shekinah is reunited with her spouse in the bridal chamber at the radiant heart of life. The evolutionary journey of the soul has been completed. She has returned home to be welcomed into the divine ground.

Because of everything that the figure of the Virgin Mary embraces, the whole past mythology of the Divine Feminine as the womb of life, as invisible soul, and as nature, this scene has crucial mythological meaning. Here, the lost feminine dimension of the Divine held in the figure of Mary is raised to relationship and union with the godhead. In Christ's gesture, as in his life, the tragic Christian tendency to dissociate nature, matter, and the body from divine spirit, because of their association with the "sin" of Eve, is dramatically and finally redeemed in a glorious affirmation of their sacredness and divinity. Only in 1950 did this image painted in the fifteenth century become doctrinally confirmed when Mary was declared by Papal Bull to be "taken up body and soul into the glory of Heaven." In 1954, Mary was pronounced Queen of Heaven, so restoring to her the ancient title of the Divine Mother.

If the meaning of this sacred marriage could become fully conscious in the human soul, there would be healing for ourselves, regeneration for our ailing civilization, and hope for the survival of the planet. If the marriage of the Divine Father-Mother, Sister-Brother, Daughter-Son could open our hearts to a new understanding of what life is, and to the utter sacredness and blazing radiance of the whole of creation, we would understand why we need to love, cherish, and protect life and each other; we would awaken to the light in which we live, move, and have our being.

There is something infinite in being the Mother of Him who is infinite.

THOMAS OF VILLANOVA

WHEN will it be that souls breathe Mary as bodies breathe the air?

LOUIS-MARIE GRIGNION DE MONTFORT
TRANSLATED BY ANDREW HARVEY

I salute you, Glorious Virgin, star more brilliant than the sun, redder than the freshest rose, whiter than any lily, higher in heaven than any of the saints. The whole earth reveres you, accept my praise and come to my aid. In the midst of your so glorious days in heaven, do not forget the miseries of this earth; turn your gaze of kindness on all those who suffer and struggle and whose lips are soaked in the bitterness of this life. Have pity on those who loved each other and were torn apart. Have pity on the loneliness of the heart, on the feebleness of our faith, on the objects of our tenderness. Have pity on those who weep, on those who pray, on those who tremble. Give everyone hopefulness and peace.

ANCIENT PRAYER OF PROTECTION
TRANSLATED BY ANDREW HARVEY

ALLELUIA! Light
Burst from your untouched
Womb like a flower
On the farther side
Of death. The world-tree
Is blossoming. Two realms become one.

HILDEGARDE OF BINGEN

For this Blessed Virgin, who was to be His Mother, God created the entire universe.

ST. BERNARD OF CLAIRVAUX

THERE is a great secret in the mystery of Mary, and that is that she IS the supreme secret of Christianity, the hidden mystery, the mystery stumbled on in rapture by those saints and mystics who opened their hearts to the darkness of her love. It is not the theologians who know Mary, but the millions of simple people who have prayed to her, and the mystics who have met her in the hidden depths of their hearts.

ANONYMOUS

_My_ soul doth magnify the Lord,
And my spirit hath rejoiced in
    God my Savior.
For he hath regarded the low estate
    of his handmaiden:
for behold, from henceforth all generations
    shall call me blessed.
For he that is mighty hath done
    to me great things; and holy is his name.
And his mercy is on them that
    fear him from generation to generation.
He hath shewed strength with his arm;
    he hath scattered the proud
    in the imagination of their hearts.
He hath put down the mighty from their
    seats, and exalted them of low degree.
He hath filled the hungry with good things;
    and the rich he hath sent empty away.
He hath holpen his servant Israel, in
    remembrance of his mercy:
As he spake to our fathers, to Abraham, and
    to his seed for ever.

LUKE 1:46–55

O VIRGIN of Virgins,
    how shall this be?
For neither before thee
    was any seen like thee,
    nor shall there be after.
Daughters of Jerusalem,
    why marvel ye at me?
The thing which ye behold
    is a divine mystery.

GREAT ANTIPHON FOR DECEMBER 23RD
FROM THE ANCIENT ENGLISH USE
IN THE _Sarum Breviary_

THE end of the earthly life of the most Holy Mother of God was the beginning of Her greatness, "being adorned with divine glory" (Ismos of the canon of the Dormition). She stands and will stand, both in the day of the last judgment and in the future age, at the right hand of the throne of her son. She reigns with Him and has boldness toward Him as His Mother according to the flesh but as one in spirit with Him, as one who performed the will of God and instructed others (Matt 5:19). Merciful and full of love, she manifests her love toward her son and God in love for the human race. She intercedes for it before the Merciful One, and going about the earth, she helps men and women. Having experienced all the difficulties of earthly life, the Intercessor of the Christian race sees every tear, hears every groan and entreaty directed to Her.

ST. JOHN MAXIMOVITCH
THE ORTHODOX VENERATION OF MARY

Hail Holy Queen
Mother of Mercy
Hail our life, our sweetness,
    and our hope.

To thee do we cry,
    poor banished children of Eve,
To thee do we send up our sighs, mourning
    and weeping
In this vale of tears.

Turn then, most gracious advocate,
    thine eyes of mercy towards us
And after this our exile, show unto us
    the blessed Fruit of thy womb, Jesus.
O merciful, O loving,
    O sweet Virgin Mary.

SALVE REGINA

THE BLESSED VIRGIN COMPARED TO THE AIR WE BREATHE

I SAY that we are wound
With mercy round and round
As if with air; the same
Is Mary, more by name.
She, wild web, wondrous robe,
Mantles the guilty globe,
Since God has let dispense
Her prayers his providence:
Nay, more than almoner,
The sweet alms' self is her
And men are meant to share
Her life as life does air...

Be thou then, O thou dear
Mother, my atmosphere;
My happier world, wherein
To wend and meet no sin;
Above me, round me lie
Fronting my forward eye
With sweet and scarless sky;
Stir in my ears, speak there
Of God's love, O live air,
Of patience, penance, prayer:
World-mothering air, air wild,
Wound with thee, in thee isled,
Fold home, fast fold thy child.

GERARD MANLEY HOPKINS

I am the Queen of Peace.
Mary is the real woman who lived
her life from her heart.
She is the symbol and archetype of
the heart itself, Mother of Divine Love.
She invites us to live from our hearts.

THE VIRGIN MARY SPEAKING AT MEDJUGORJE:
AUGUST 6, 1981

ETERNAL Wisdom builds;
May I become her palace
For She has found in me
and I in Her all Peace.

ANGELUS SILESIUS
TRANSLATED BY ANDREW HARVEY

I have come to tell the world that God is
truth: He exists. True happiness and the
fullness of life are in God. I have come here
as Queen of Peace to tell the world that
peace is necessary for the salvation of the
world. In God, you find true joy from which
true peace springs naturally. In the power of
love you can do even those things that seem
impossible for you. Hatred creates division
and does not see anybody or thing...Carry
unity and peace...Act with love in the place
where you live. Let love always be your only
tool. With love turn everything to good.

THE VIRGIN MARY SPEAKING AT MEDJUGORJE

To find the grace of God, you have to find Mary. It is she who has given being and life to the source of all grace, and so she is called the Mother of Grace...God has chosen Her for the treasurer, gatherer, and dispenser of all His graces. All His graces and gifts pass by her hands.

LOUIS-MARIE GRIGNION DE MONTFORT
TRANSLATED BY ANDREW HARVEY

These are the times of the great return. Yes, after the time of the great suffering, there will be the time of the great rebirth and all will blossom again.

Humanity will again be a new garden of life and of beauty.

THE VIRGIN MARY SPEAKING AT MEDJUGORJE:
MARCH 25, 1986

You are the shimmering lily
Which God knew
Before all other creatures.

O most beautiful, most tender one,
How deep was God's delight in you
When on you He placed
The heat of His embrace
So that by you His Son
    could be suckled.

What ecstasy your womb knew
When all heaven's harmony
Rang out from you
For you bore the son of God
When your purity blazed on God.

HILDEGARDE OF BINGEN
TRANSLATED BY ANDREW HARVEY

WE see the Holy Virgin as a flaming torch appearing to those in darkness. For having kindled the Immaterial Light, she leads all to divine knowledge: she illumines our minds with radiance and is honored by our shouting these praises:

Rejoice, ray of the spiritual sun!
Rejoice, flash of unfading splendor!
Rejoice, lightning that lights up our lives!

FROM EIKOS II OF THE AKATHIST HYMN TO THE VIRGIN

REJOICE, flaming symbol of the
    Resurrection!
Rejoice, mirror of the life of
    the Angels!
Rejoice, tree of glorious fruit by which
    the faithful are nourished!

FROM EIKOS I OF THE AKATHIST HYMN TO THE VIRGIN

Mary is everywhere the true tree that bears
the fruit of life, and the real mother that
produces it.

LOUIS-MARIE GRIGNION DE MONTFORT
TRANSLATED BY ANDREW HARVEY

THESE are the Virgin's names:
    a throne, God's canopy,
Ark, fortress, tower, house, garden,
    mirror, fountain,
The sea, a star, the moon, the rose of
    dawn, a mountain:
She is another world, so can be all
    these things freely.

ANGELUS SILESIUS
TRANSLATED BY ANDREW HARVEY

Rejoice, Depth hard to
    contemplate even for the eyes
    of angels!
Rejoice, you who are the king's throne!
Rejoice, you who bear Him who
    bears all!
Rejoice, star that causes the Sun
    to appear!
Rejoice, womb of the divine
    Incarnation!
Rejoice, you through whom the
    creation becomes new!

FROM EIKOS I OF THE AKATHIST HYMN TO THE VIRGIN

MADONNA AND CHILD SEATED, CHILD HOLDING A BIRD

After *Pierfrancesco da Fiorentino* fl. 1470–1500

CHAPTER NINE

MERCY AND COMPASSION

Islam

And your God is one God:
there is no God but The One,
the Compassionate,
the Merciful.

THE KORAN

*A*t the very core of Islamic philosophy there are glowing traces of what can be called a vision of the Motherhood of God. In the first "sura" of the Koran — the famous "fatiha" that is recited by millions in their devotions every day — God is called *al-rahmin*, the merciful and compassionate one. *Rahmin* derives from the Arabic for "womb" or "matrix," and the mercy of God is clearly meant to be thought of as a feminine attribute. God to the Muslim is both *jamal* and *jalal*, both tender and terrible. The Koran, when you read it carefully, is as full of visions of God's wonderful gentleness toward human beings and His amazing providential care of them in every way, and of examples of the vast loving-kindness of God's heart, as it is of visions of hell-fire, judgment, violence, and furious admonishments. Muhammad himself, constantly and with wonderful sweetness of soul, stressed God's infinite capacity for

forgiveness: the courtesy with which Muhammad treated his enemies shows how deeply he had learned his own lesson.

The contemporary fanaticism of much of Islam is in fact anti-Koranic; the Koran makes it clear in several passages that everyone who lives a life of holy reverence is welcomed into Paradise, whatever their religion. Muhammad is full of praise for both Judaism (Abraham is revered in the Koran as deeply as in the Old Testament) and for Jesus – his love for Jesus and his honoring of Jesus's sublime message radiates throughout the Koran. This "Mother" tolerance of other faiths was in fact characteristic of Islam in its great age, in medieval Spain and Egypt, for example. Perhaps only Buddhism has been as tolerant or as embracing of the truths of others as Islam was in its classical period.

Another surprise that awaits anyone who studies the Koran is the Koranic reverence for Mary, the mother of Christ. Very few Christians know that Mary is considered by the Prophet to be the very greatest and highest adept of all – the most marvelous of all women. She is considered, both in the Koran and later in theological commentaries on it, to have reached the very summit of "servanthood" (in Arabic *ubuda*) and to be the greatest possible example to any believer of the transforming and life-giving power of pure selfless adoration of the Divine. In later Koranic commentaries, Mary emerges as the supreme veil let down by Allah between himself and humankind, the supreme veil of Allah's mercy, forgiveness, sweetness, and humility toward his creatures, the supreme sign of the loving-kindness of God.

When the Prophet reentered Mecca and started to cleanse the Kaaba of the images and frescoes that "sullied" it, he left on the wall the fresco of the Virgin and her child. In one of the most luminous and enigmatic of *hadiths* (prophetic sayings), the Prophet is reported to have said, "Paradise is at the feet of the Mothers." What can this mean but that the feminine qualities of adoration, intuition, capacity for surrender, and infinite cherishing of life in all its forms are the gateways to supreme consciousness?

The "feminine" side of Muhammad's experience of the Divine may have been shelved or severely clouded over in exoteric "official" Islam; however, its power and radiance continued in the esoteric aspects of Islam, most notably of course in the glorious poetry and philosophy of the Sufis. Sufism can be defined in many ways, but it is primarily and marvelously a path of the heart – a way of passion, of adoration. For the Sufis, the Divine is considered the beloved, infinitely majestic and infinitely blissful and tender, and the entire aim of Sufi mystical discipline is to open the human heart – through prayer and the recitation of the sacred names of God as well as meditation and dreamwork - to this infinite beauty that is its own secret identity and power. A great Indian mystic, Meerabai, said, "All men are women before the Absolute." No mystical tradition has cultivated the feminine virtues of tender adoration, receptive to the Presence in all living things and events, as whole-souledly as the Sufis. One way of imagining the Divine Feminine is to see it as the path of the lover – the lover of divine human life, the lover of divine human love and all its revelatory splendors, the lover of the wonder of so-called ordinary experience known and lived in its divine ecstatic dimension. Sufi mysticism gives to all lovers of the Divine Feminine the clearest, richest, wildest, most poignant and passionate vision of the path of the lover. "Wherever you are," Rumi wrote, "and in whatever circumstances, try always to be a lover and a passionate lover. Once you have possessed love, you will remain a lover in the tomb, on the day of Resurrection, in Paradise and forever." He also wrote, "You must be alive in love for a dead man can do nothing. Who is alive? He to whom love gives birth."

One of the greatest strengths of the Sufi vision is its unsentimental understanding of what such a birth of love into its truth really entails. It entails nothing less than a surrender to every necessary ordeal, every ordained devastation, the commitment – which can be called feminine – never to evade suffering in the pursuit of truth. Listen to Rumi and his "feminine" awareness of the process and price of this birth:

As long as Mary did not feel the pain of childbirth, she did not
go toward the tree of blessing. The pangs of childbirth drew her to
the trunk of the palm tree. Pain took her to the tree and the barren
tree bore fruit. This body is like Mary, and each of us has a Jesus
inside us. If the pain appears, our Jesus will be born. If no pain
arrives, Jesus will return to origin by the same secret way that He
came, and we will be deprived of Him and reap no joy.

Such a realistic embrace of the necessity of suffering in the process of birth brings
us into the heart of the mystery of the Divine Feminine. The price of living and
embodying the Divine, of entering and radiating love, of living with no fear or
barrier the human divine life, aware at once of its transcendent and immanent
aspects, is a very high one; it involves the acceptance, as the greatest Sufi mystics
remind us again and again, of death after death, the brave acceptance of pain as
essential to purification and as essential to the alchemical transformation of the
dull human mind and heart into their secret gold. As Rumi wrote:

How much the Beloved made me suffer before the Work
Grew entwined inseparably with blood and eyes!
A thousand grim fires and heartbreaks –
And its name is "Love" –
A thousand pains and regrets and attacks
And its name is "Beloved"…
Heartbreak is a treasure because it contains mercies
The kernel is soft when the rind is scraped off;
O Brother, the place of darkness and cold
Is the fountain of life and the cup of ecstasy.

There is nothing morbid or masochistic about such a vision; the Sufi does not run to suffering out of a neurotic self-hatred or secret hunger for punishment, but neither does he or she run from it. A Sufi knows, in Attar's words, "There is no Resurrection without the Crucifixion," that there is no *baqa* (subsistence in the Divine Ground) without *fana* (the annihilation of the false self and its fantasies). One of the greatest, most transforming, of all the gifts of the Divine Feminine is the knowledge of how to open to suffering without masochism but also without fear, with a deep, blind, dark, fertile trust in its ordained necessity and in the hand of mercy that is always – even in the most extreme circumstances – dispensing it. Only an acceptance of its terms can help love to give birth to the new divine human child "at the feet of the Mothers."

The Sufi mystics are supreme masters of this knowledge of suffering, because they are supreme masters of the alchemical "science" of love. And what is the path of the Mother but the path of love? And how can pain be avoided on that path, especially in a time like ours, when to open to the facts of what is happening to our psyches and to the environment is to open inevitably to agony and horror and the prospect of ultimate catastrophe? In such an opening to the full pain of the facts and the full pain of real transformation, the Sufi mystics, with their profound understanding of the nature of adoration and of the transforming mercy of accepted heartbreak, can be extraordinary and helpful "midwives" of a new possibility.

The heart, everyone's heart, is longing to give birth; and giving birth, becoming a "mother" of our own divine self, is the aim of human life. Accepting the price of this birth of fearlessness is the courage of the Divine Feminine, the supreme inner courage of the mystic, and leads to what the Sufis know as the ultimate state of union with reality, of being able to "dance" with adoration and nondual bliss in all dimensions simultaneously. And as Rumi reminds us, with the authentic passion and realism of the Divine Feminine, "Dancing is not raising your feet painlessly like a whirl of dust blown about by the wind. Dancing is when you rise above both worlds, tearing your heart to pieces and giving up your soul."

EVE FROM A TURKISH MINIATURE OF 1595

In that moment you are drunk on yourself,
The friend seems a thorn,
In that moment you leap free of yourself,
    what use is the friend?
In that moment you are drunk on yourself,
You are the prey of a mosquito,
And the moment you leap free of yourself,
    you go elephant hunting.
In that moment you are drunk on yourself,
You lock yourself away in cloud after
    cloud of grief,
And in that moment you leap
    free of yourself,
The moon catches you and hugs you
    in its arms.
That moment you are drunk on yourself,
    the friend abandons you.
That moment you leap free of yourself,
    the wine of the friend,
In all its brilliance and dazzle,
    is held out to you.
That moment you are drunk on yourself,
You are withered, withered like
    autumn leaves.
That moment you leap free of yourself,
Winter to you appears in the dazzling
    robes of spring.
All disquiet springs from the
    search for quiet.
Look for disquiet and you will come
    suddenly on a field of quiet.

All illnesses spring from the
    scavenging for delicacies.
Renounce delicacies and poison itself will
    seem delicious to you.
All disappointments spring from your
    hunting for satisfactions.
If only you could stop, all imaginable joys
Would be rolled like pearls to your feet.
Be passionate for the friend's tyranny,
    not his tenderness,
So the arrogant beauty in you can become
    a lover that weeps.
When the king of the feast, Shams-ud-Din,
    arrives from Tabriz,
God knows you'll be ashamed then of the
    moon and stars.

RUMI
TRANSLATED BY ANDREW HARVEY

LOVE'S APOCALYPSE, LOVE'S GLORY

O NE breath from the breath of the
    lover would be enough to burn
    away the world
To scatter this insignificant universe
    like grains of sand.
The whole of the cosmos would
    become a Sea,
And sacred terror rubble this
    Sea to nothing.

No human being would remain,
and no creature:
A smoke would come from heaven:
there would be no more man
or angel:
Out of this smoke, flame would
suddenly flash out across heaven.
That second, the sky would split
apart and neither space nor
existence remain.
Vast groans would rise up out of the
breast of the universe,
groans mingled with desolate
moaning,
And fire eat up water, and water
eat up fire:
The waves of the Sea of the Void would
drown in their flood
the horseman of day and night:
The sun itself fades, vanishes, before this
flaming-out of the soul of man.
Do not ask anyone who is not intimate
with the secrets
When the intimate of the secret himself
cannot answer you.
Mars will lose its swagger, Jupiter burn
the book of the world,
The moon will not hold its empire,
its joy will be smirched with agony,
Mercury will shipwreck in mud,
Saturn burn itself to death;

Venus, singer of heaven, play no longer
her songs of joy.
The rainbow will flee, and the cup,
and the wine,
Thee will be no more happiness or
rapture, no more wound or cure,
Water will no longer dance with light,
wind no longer sweep the ground,
Gardens no longer abandon themselves
to laughter, April's clouds no longer
scatter their dew.
There will be no more grief, no more
consolation, no more "enemy"
or "witness,"
No more flute or song, or lute or
mode, no more high or low pitch.
Causes will faint away: the cupbearer
will serve himself,
The soul will recite, "O my Lord most
high": the heart will cry out,
"My Lord knows best."
Rise up! The painter of Eternity has
set to work one more time
To trace miraculous figures on the
crazy curtain of the world.
God has lit a fire to burn the heart
of the universe,
The Sun of God has the East for a
heart: the splendor of that East
Irradiates at all moments the son of
Adam, Jesus, son of Mary.

RUMI
TRANSLATED BY ANDREW HARVEY

128

THE VALLEY OF LOVE

Love's valley is the next,
    and here desire
Will plunge the pilgrim into
    seas of fire,
Until his very being is enflamed
And those whom fire rejects
    turn back ashamed.
The lover is a man who flares
    and burns
Whose face is fevered,
    who in frenzy yearns,
Who knows no prudence,
    who will gladly send
A hundred worlds toward their
    blazing end,
Who knows of neither faith
    nor blasphemy,
Who has no time for doubt
    or certainty,
To whom both good and evil
    are the same,
And who is neither, but a living flame...
Love here is fire; its thick smoke clouds
    the head —
When love has come the
    intellect has fled;
It cannot tutor love, and all its care
Supplies no remedy for love's despair.
If you could seek the unseen you would find
Love's home, which is not reason

or the mind,
And love's intoxication tumbles down
The world's designs for glory
    and renown —
If you could penetrate their
    passing show
And see the world's wild atoms,
    you would know
That reason's eyes will never
    glimpse one spark
Of shining love to mitigate the dark.
Love leads whoever starts
    along our Way;
The noblest bow to love
    and must obey —
But you, unwilling both
    to love and tread
The pilgrim's path, you might
    as well be dead!
The lover chafes, impatient to depart,
And longs to sacrifice
    his life and heart.

FROM ATTAR "CONFERENCE OF THE BIRDS"
TRANSLATED BY DICK DAVIS

MOTHERS

Mother of the Living, the beloved Eve, may the Peace of Allah always be upon her, received on her gentle brow the shining Light of Prophecy after the passing away of the first holy Prophet on earth, the beloved Adam, may the Peace of Allah always be upon him. The All-Forgiving One turned His Glory toward our original father and mother, washing their hearts in the purifying and healing stream of la ilaha illallah, fulfilling their longing to experience mystic union, and focusing His Divine Light and His Divine Word through them for the guidance of all future humanity.

From the sacred brow of our holy mother Eve, the Light of Revelation descended through countless generations of Prophets until the appearance of the second supreme mother of humanity, confirmed in the Glorious Koran as a channel of Divine Love to all human beings until the end of time, our sublime spiritual mother, the beloved Mary, may the Peace of Allah always be upon her. Mary the Illumined courageously accepted the virgin birth of the ruhullah, the very Spirit of Allah, the beloved Jesus, may Divine Peace embrace him and be transmitted through him to all his lovers throughout history...

Finally, the manifestation of Divine Attributes through the feminine form of humanity reached its culmination in the one who does not fit into any books or words, the majestic Fatima, may the secret of her union with Allah and with the Prophet of Allah be revealed and replicated in all mature hearts. The noble Messenger proclaimed unequivocally of the august Fatima, "she is part of my prophecy." The sublime Ali, Whirling Lion of Allah, most mature among the spiritually mature, recognized our holy mother Fatima as the inward successor of the Prophet of Allah in the mystical lineage hidden within the secret heart of Islam. He therefore did not take hand with the first Khalifa, Abu Bakr the Truthful, until, after six months of unimaginable yearning, the brilliant light of the soul of Fatima left this surface world to join the soul of her father in the Garden of Essence, where there is only one soul.

Our most profound and humble greeting, salaams, and kisses to the earth where the feet of these holy mothers have walked: beloved Eve, beloved Mary, most precious Khadija, most precious Aisha, and the Pearl Beyond Price — the majestic and mysterious mother of the Mirror of the Prophet, the noble Hussain, may the Peace of Allah always be upon him, the Mother of the

Ecstatic Lovers, Supreme Lover and Beloved of the Prophet – Fatima the Enlightened.

The mothers of all humanity are reflected in these radiant Mothers of the Faithful. When asked who is the most important person for the soul, the noble Prophet responded thrice, with decisive intensity, by repeating the sacred word mother. The Holder of Spiritual Secrets reveals in his Oral Tradition the mysterious words, "Paradise abides at the feet of the mothers." The holy tomb of Fatima the True Secret, contained in the house of the Prophet that is embraced within the Grand Mosque in Medina the Illumined, surges with a flood of spiritual power, which inundates the earth with subtle blessings. This radiant energy of love, flowing from Fatima's fragrant resting-place, is not separate in any way from the baraka, the transforming holiness streaming from the Tomb of tombs, the refreshing Palace of Love's Resurrection, the resting-place of the beloved Muhammad. This oasis of Love is also the destined resting-place of the beloved Jesus, after he returns and reigns over the entire globe. Here the two Prophets of Love and intimate spiritual brothers in Divine Love will manifest side by side on earth, as they do now in the highest Circle of Love.

FROM *Atom from the Sun of Knowledge*
BY LEX HIXON

THE mystery of motherhood shines as Mecca, Mother of Holy Places, radiates as the Glorious Koran, Mother of Scriptures, and illumines the entire universe as *umma*, the spiritual community, Mother of the Lovers of Truth. The mystery of motherhood sparkles secretly as the primary Divine Names, *rahman* and *rahim*, which derive from the single Arabic root meaning *womb*. The mystery of motherhood glows delicately as the spiritual pregnancy of the heart of both men and women along the mystic way. This rich spiritual mystery manifests in a special sense through all women.

O Matrix of Existence!

O Birthgiver, Educator,
    and Protector of all Worlds!

O Glorious One!

Amin amin alhamdulillahi
    rabbi-l-alamin.

FROM *Atom from the Sun of Knowledge*
BY LEX HIXON

SAY I AM YOU

I am dust particles in sunlight.
I am the round sun.

To the bits of dust I say, Stay.
To the sun, Keep moving.

I am morning mist,
and the breathing of evening.

I am wind in the top of a grove,
and surf on the cliff.

Mast, rudder, helmsman, and keel,
I am also the coral reef they founder on.

I am a tree with a trained parrot
*   in its branches.*
Silence, thought, and voice.

The musical air coming through a
flute, a spark of a stone, a flickering

in metal. Both candle,
and the moth crazy around it.

Rose, and the nightingale
lost in the fragrance.

I am all orders of being, the circling galaxy,
the evolutionary intelligence, the lift,

and the falling away. What is,
and what isn't. You who know

Jelaluddin, You the one
in all, say who

I am.
Say I am You.

RUMI
TRANSLATED BY COLEMAN BARKS

W HEN I stand for prayer,
I intend to prolong it, but on hearing
cries of children, I cut it short,
as I dislike to trouble the mothers.

FROM *Atom from the Sun of Knowledge*
BY LEX HIXON

May the eyes of the heart of both men and women be opened to the inspiring spiritual reality of motherhood, the startling spiritual implications of motherhood, the enlightening spiritual secrets of motherhood.

FROM *Atom from the Sun of Knowledge*
BY LEX HIXON

THIS world is nothing more than
Beauty's chance to show Herself.
And what are we? —
Nothing more than Beauty's
   chance to see Herself.
For if Beauty were not seeking Herself
   we would not exist.

Every particle of creation sings its own
   song of what is, and what is not.
The wise hear what is.
The mad hear what is not.
And only a cracked mirror will show
   a difference.

All your knowledge leads you in
   the wrong direction;
All your worship only puts you to
   sleep.
Insipid is this world which only
   believes in what is seen;
Here, taste the wine from this Cup
   which cannot be seen...

On account of those who repeat His
   Name.
The Earth has become a paradise,
   an honored place in the order of
   creation.
God's love is on this Earth,
And the heavens forever bend
   over to greet Her.

GHALIB
TRANSLATED BY JONATHAN STAR

CHAPTER TEN

MOTHER OF COMPASSION

Buddhism

From my heart I bow to the Holy Lady, essence of compassion,
the three unerring and precious places of refuge gathered into one:
until I gain the terrace of enlightenment
I pray you grasp me with the iron hook of your compassion.

LAMA LOZANG TENPE JETS'EN
HYMN TO TARA

*O*ut of the Buddha's Enlightenment in Bodh Gaya in c. 480 B.C. arose a vision and
a vast and glorious body of spiritual teachings that were to transform the face of
Asia and have immense and still unfolding consequences for millions of individuals as
well as the history of the world. Both in its original Hinayana (or "Lesser Vehicle")
form and in its later Mahayana ("Greater Vehicle") development, the religion of
Buddhism came to offer a philosophy of living that a large part of Asia could take to
its heart – a philosophy at once fierce and compassionate, unsentimental and soberly
ecstatic, practical and metaphysical. Everything – the ethics, spiritual techniques, and
art of a whole continent – was to be profoundly changed by the Buddha's great
teaching and the example of his holy life.

At first glance there are aspects of Buddhism that do not seem especially favorable to the restoration of the Divine Feminine. The teachings of the Buddha, as handed down to us in the Dhammapada, are sometimes chillingly ascetic; the Buddha himself left his wife and son to pursue the spiritual life and seems to have viewed the world and its relationships, and the body itself, as unsatisfactory and a burden. From the beginning, Buddhism's relationship with women was problematical; the Buddha only reluctantly allowed women to be ordained and then claimed that their ordination would halve the life of the Dharma. Traditional Buddhism, like most religions, is dominated by men, in imagery, practice, institutions, income, and prestige, and this "male bias" extends also to the language and some of the major philosophical emphases of the teachings. Nevertheless, if Buddhism and its teachings are looked at deeply, it can be seen that there is a core of teaching of the Divine Feminine running through and often transforming the harsher "masculine" aspects of the Dharma.

The Buddha himself was "saved" and instructed by the Divine Feminine at two crucial moments in his journey. The first came when he was engaged in ruthless ascetic practices that were threatening his health and sanity. A woman named Sugata came with a bowl of curds, and instead of continuing with this "discipline," the Buddha accepted and ate them. From this gesture of a woman came the Buddha's realization of the necessity of a Middle Way that did not extinguish the body entirely, but honored balance in all its form, and recognized a wise "feminine" balance between all extremes as essential to the enlightened life.

The second meeting with the Divine Feminine occurs near the end of the Buddha's journey into enlightenment. Assaulted by Mara, the King of Demons, who threw against the Buddha every illusion and fantasy in his armory, the Buddha put his right hand down and touched the earth and begged the divine Mother of Earth, Rani, to come to his aid. She did so, and a flood from her hair erased and wiped out all the "powers" that had been thrown against him. This calling of the earth to witness his inner truth was a crucial step for the Buddha; it was a choice to ground

TARA, THE DIVINE MOTHER OF TIBETAN BUDDHISM

his awakening, to enter reality and not escape from it. By opening his entire being to the nature of Divine Feminine reality, the Buddha achieved in himself the sacred marriage between heaven and earth, masculine and feminine, wisdom and compassion.

While the sex- and body-hating aspects of some of the Buddha's teaching cannot be denied, what is also undeniable is that this teaching has at its core a very profound understanding and advocacy of compassion as the only possible wise response to life and living beings. The statues that convey – or try to – something of the Buddha's presence always have a certain radiant androgyny, and all the accounts of his personality stress marvelous gentleness and tenderness toward all life, including animal life. The Buddha's poignant sense of the suffering of all sentient beings flowered into a philosophy and practice of compassion that enfolded all living things in an

unconditional embrace and acceptance. That the nature of this compassion was
recognized and celebrated as feminine is made clear in the early Sutta Nipata Sutra,
which claims to hand on the Buddha's own teaching on loving kindness:

May creatures all abound in weal and peace
May all be blessed with peace always.
Let none cajole or flout
His fellow anywhere
Let none wish others harm
In dudgeon or hate.
Just as with her own life, a mother
Shields from hurt her own, her only child,
Let all-embracing thoughts
For all that lives be thine —
An all-embracing love for all the universe
In all its heights and depths and breadth,
Unstinted love, unmarred by hate within…

This magnificent vision of compassion, of "an all-embracing love for the
universe…unmarred by hate within," is the deathless contribution of Buddhism to the
religious imagination of the world. In mystical elaborations of this compassion – in
the Mahayana vision of the Mother of Compassion, in the evolution of a female
savior named Tara, in the Tantric sexual and philosophical vision that embraces sex
and the holiness of women – we find developments of the Buddha's teachings that
expand the Divine Feminine truths already inherent in them.

Let us take, to begin with, the later Mahayana vision of supreme wisdom being
the "Mother" of all things, including authentic compassion. It is one of the greatest
strengths of the Buddha's teachings that he views compassion and wisdom as
essentially one at the highest level. Compassion is not merely an emotional response
to the suffering and need of beings; it arises out of the revelation that supreme

wisdom (Prajnaparamita) alone can "mother" (give birth to) an understanding of the "emptiness" of all phenomena. Milarepa crystalized this teaching in his statement, "Seeing emptiness, have compassion." What the Buddha invites us to do is to let go of all the structures and concepts that inhibit our awareness of our inherent nonexistence, or, putting it differently, of our "interdependence" with every other thing that exists, so that we can be released from all suffering that comes from a mistaken narrow belief in one identity and also cultivate intense compassion for all others caught in its imaginary hell. All words, structures, dogmas, formulations, and conceptions are "empty"; when this is realized beyond thought we are initiated into the ground of our being, which is that shining boundless void of wisdom and compassion that is the Mother of all reality, and so, of all true awakening. That this experience of the void is an experience of the Mother of all things is made clear in hymn after hymn in the Mahayana tradition. Take Rahula Sadra's wonderful celebration:

Homage to Thee, Perfect Wisdom,
Boundless, and transcending thought,
All thy limbs are without blemish,
Faultless those who thee discern.

Spotless, unobstructed, silent,
Like the vast expanse of space;
Who in truth does really see Thee
The Tathagata perceives.

As the moonlight does not differ
From the moon, so also Thou

Who abounds in holy virtues
Are the Teacher of the world ...

Teachers of the world, the Buddhas
Are thine own compassionate sons;
They art Thou, O Blessed Lady,
Grandmother thus of beings all.

All the immaculate perfections
At all times encircle Thee
As the stars surround the crescent,
O Thou blameless holy one!

To realize the voidness of phenomena then is to realize the immense "spotless, unobstructed, silent," all-embracing nature of supreme wisdom, the Mother of all phenomena. To awaken to this sublime, all-cradling Mother truth is to give birth to the supreme virtues needed for the freedom of enlightenment – fearlessness, boundless stamina, indefatigable concern, and commitment to liberate all beings from their prisons of false understanding. As Lex Hixon writes in *Mother of the Buddhas*, his vibrant re-creation of the Prajnaparamita Sutra:

> *I sing this spontaneous hymn of light to praise Mother Prajnaparamita. She is worthy of infinite praise. She is utterly unstained, because nothing in this insubstantial world can possibly stain her. She is an ever-flowing fountain of incomparable light…She leads living beings into her clear light from the blindness and obscurity caused by moral and spiritual impurity as well as by partial or distorted views of reality…Mother Prajnaparamita is total awakeness. She never substantially creates any limited structure because she experiences none of the tendencies of living beings to grasp, project, or conceptualize…She is the Perfect Wisdom that never comes into being and therefore never goes out of being. She is known as the Great Mother by those spiritually mature beings who dedicate their mind streams to the liberation and full enlightenment of all that lives.*

Perhaps because such a concept was too abstract for many people, there gradually grew up within Mahayana Buddhism a need for a female figure to crystalize such intuitions about the feminine face of reality. This figure came to be Tara, the Savioress, whose name means Star. Veneration of Tara seems to have begun around the seventh or eighth century in India. It was then imported into Tibet by Atisa, who arrived there in 1042, and it became a potent spiritual force in Tibet by the fourteenth century and continued to grow in intensity until the present day. The worship of the Goddess Tara is now one of the most widespread of Tibetan cults, unaffected by sect, education, class, or position; from the highest to the lowest, the Tibetans realize with Tara a personal and enduring relationship, unmatched by any other single deity, even among those of their gods more powerful in appearance or seemingly more profound in symbolic association. Tara, in other words, is the Divine Mother of Tibetan Buddhism, a tender, beautiful, intimately and personally concerned deity who protects all who turn to her from what is called in tradition, the eight great terrors – drowning, thieves, lions, snakes, fire, spirit, captivity, and elephants – and also from the sixteen great terrors that include the eight already mentioned and add doubt, lust, avarice, envy, false views, hatred, delusion, and pride. As an ancient Tibetan prayer ends:

> *I pay homage to Tara, the Mother*
> *Who saves us from all poverty and danger*
> *May I and all sentient beings*
> *Live directly in your sublime presence.*

In some of the many beautiful stories that have come down to us, merely saying Tara's name brings her instant help. In Tibet, the power of her mantra – Om Tara Tuttare Ture Svaha – when repeated in the heart with devotion is universally recognized. Gedundrub, a great devotee of the Goddess, writes; "If one knows enough to recite her mantra, then it is said though one's head be cut off, one will live, though one's flesh be hacked to pieces, one will live;

THE TARA DEVIS

this is a profound counsel." Another lover of Tara, Dorje Chopa, has written, "The recitation of her mantra has great consequences…just sharing its sound has inconceivable effect that saves from suffering whatever one wants to have, whatever unpleasant thing one wants to be without, she responds to it like an echo. Tara loves and protects the practitioner as if she were the moon accompanying him, never a step away."

Another, recently revealed aspect of the Buddhist development of the Divine Feminine is that of the Indian Tantric Buddhist tradition. Miranda Shaw's pioneering work *Passionate Enlightenment* revives forty unnoticed works by women of the Pala period, from the eighth through the twelfth centuries, and radically reinterprets that crucial aspect of Buddhist history. She demonstrates how important the vision of these Tantric women adepts is for us today, when women everywhere are reclaiming their power, and the revolution of the Divine Feminine is opening up to humanity a vision of a holy liberating sexuality, free of shame, fear, and body-hatred.

This extraordinary Tantric tradition "rewrote" the conventional history of the Buddha's spiritual journey; according to it, the Buddha did not really achieve enlightenment at Bodh Gaya, his journey and his self-discipline were a display to impress ordinary people. The Tantric tradition claims that the Buddha was in fact enlightened by the bliss that he experienced with his wife Gopa, long before he set out on his journey. As it is written in the Cabdamaharosanatantra:

> *Along with Gopa, [the Buddha] experienced bliss.*
> *By uniting the diamond scepter and lotus*
> *He attained the fruit of bliss.*
> *Buddahood is obtained from bliss, and*
> *Apart from women there will not be bliss.*

Such a radical reinterpretation of the conventional story led inevitably to a religious glorification of women and the feminine. A man who undertook Tantric practice in this tradition was asked to envisage his female partner as a goddess and to pay her homage with his whole being – emotional, spiritual, and physical. Such devotion, when combined with a deep meditational awareness of the Prajnaparamita, of the nature of emptiness, leads, the tradition claimed, to the experience of nondual bliss and compassionate ecstasy that is enlightenment. As the goddess Vajrayogini instructs the woman in the Tantric couple to say to her male partner:

Constantly take refuge at my feet, my dear
Be gracious, beloved and
Give me pleasure with your diamond scepter
Look at my three petaled lotus
Its center adorned with a stamen
It is a Buddha paradise, adorned with a red Buddha,
A cosmic mother who bestows
Bliss and tranquility on the passionate.

Nothing is more important for the restoration of the Divine Feminine than the rediscovery and holy reenactment of this wonderful tradition, and its sister traditions in Taoism, Kabbalah, and Hinduism. In the rediscovery of the liberating power of sexuality, when combined with a meditative understanding of "emptiness" and universal compassion, lie as yet unimaginable possibilities for freedom and blessings and for that sanctification of human life in all of its holy particulars and activities that is the goal, and gift, of the Divine Feminine.

MOTHER OF THE BUDDHAS

Unthinkably deep is the loving commitment of Buddhas and bodhisattvas to Mother Prajnaparamita — cherishing her, protecting her and receiving her protection. She is their true nature, matrix, guide, power, and bliss. She alone has revealed unobstructed and spontaneous omniscience to them as total awakeness. She has patiently instructed them to deal skilfully with the empty, transparent nature of existence, tenderly awakening all living beings from the dream of individuality, substantiality, and separation. From her compassion and wisdom alone have the Tathagatas miraculously come forth. She alone shows them the world as it really is. The pure presence of the Awakened Ones comes from her and is simply her plenitude. All Buddhas from the beginningless past, from the infinite dimensions of the present, and from the inconceivable expanse of the future reach full enlightenment thanks to their one universal Wisdom Mother.

FROM *Mother of the Buddhas*
BY LEX HIXON

SACRED COMPASSION

I WOULD be a protector for those without protection, a leader for those who journey, and a boat, a bridge, a passage for those desiring the further shore.

For all creatures, I would be a lantern for those desiring a lantern, I would be a bed for those desiring a bed, I would be a slave for those desiring a slave.

I would be for creatures a magic jewel, an inexhaustible jar, a powerful spell, an universal remedy, a wishing tree, and a cow of plenty.

As the earth and other elements are, in various ways, for the enjoyment of innumerable beings dwelling in all of space;

So may I be, in various ways, the means of sustenance for the living beings occupying space, for as long a time as all are not satisfied.

As the ancient Buddhas seized the Thought of Enlightenment, and in like manner they followed regularly on the path of Bodhisattva instruction,

Thus also do I cause the Thought of Enlightenment to arise for the welfare of the world, and thus shall I practice these instructions in proper order.

The wise man, having considered serenely the Thought of Enlightenment, should rejoice, for the sake of its growth and its well-being, in the thought:

Today my birth is completed, my human nature is most appropriate; today I have been born into the Buddha-family and I am now a Buddha-son.

It is now for me to behave according to the customary behavior of one's own family, in order that there may be no stain put upon that spotless family.

As a blind man may obtain a jewel in a heap of dust, so, somehow, this Thought of Enlightenment has arisen even within me.

This elixir has originated for the destruction of death in the world. It is the imperishable treasure which alleviates the world's poverty.

It is the uttermost medicine, the abatement of the world's disease. It is a tree of rest for the wearied world journeying on the road of being.

When crossing over hard places, it is the universal bridge for all travelers. It is the risen moon of mind (*citta*), the soothing of the world's hot passion (*klesa*).

It is a great sun dispelling the darkness of the world's ignorance. It is fresh butter, surging up from the

churning of the milk of the true
Dharma.

For the caravan of humanity, moving
along the road of being, hungering for
the enjoyment of happiness, this
happiness banquet is prepared for the
complete refreshening of every being
who comes to it.

SHANTIDEVA BODHICHARYAVATARA
TRANSLATED BY MATICS

HYMN TO TARA

Lady whose eyes flash like lightning,
heroine, TARE, TUTTARE,
born from the corolla of the lotus
of the Buddha's face: to you I bow.
Lady whose face is like the circle
of the full autumn moon,
lady who grasps a lotus flower
with the gift-bestowing gesture,
homage to you!
From the cage of this world TUTTARE!
Pacifying defilements with SVAHA!
With OM by your very essence
opening the gate of Brahma: to you I bow.
Protecting the entire world
from the eight great terrors,
Blessed Lady, mother of all,
homage to Tara, the mother!

VAGISVARAKIRTI

HOMAGE TO TARA

Homage to Tara our mother:
great compassion!

Homage to Tara our mother:
a thousand hands, a thousand eyes!

Homage to Tara our mother:
queen of physicians!

Homage to Tara our mother:
conquering disease like medicine!

Homage to Tara our mother:
knowing the means of compassion!

Homage to Tara our mother:
a foundation like the earth!

Homage to Tara our mother:
cooling like water!

Homage to Tara our mother:
ripening like fire!

Homage to Tara our mother:
spreading like wind!

Homage to Tara our mother:
pervading like space!

ANCIENT BUDDHIST HYMN

Sariputra: Goddess, what prevents you from transforming yourself out of your female state?

Goddess: Although I have sought my "female state" for these twelve years, I have not yet found it. Reverend Sariputra, if a magician were to incarnate a woman by magic, would you ask her, "What prevents you from transforming yourself out of your female state?"

Sariputra: No! Such a woman would not really exist, so what would there be to transform?

Goddess: Just so, reverend Sariputra, all things do not really exist. Now, would you think, "What prevents one whose nature is that of a magical incarnation from transforming herself out of her female state?"

Thereupon, the goddess employed her magical power to cause the elder Sariputra to appear in her form and to cause herself to appear in his form. Then the goddess, transformed into Sariputra, said to Sariputra, transformed into a goddess, "Reverend Sariputra, what prevents you from transforming yourself out of your female state?"

And Sariputra, transformed into the goddess, replied, "I no longer appear in the form of a male! My body has changed into the body of a woman! I do not know what to transform!"

The goddess continued, "If the elder could change out of the female state, then all women could also change out of their female states. All women appear in the form of women in just the same way as the elder appears in the form of a woman. While they are not women in reality, they appear in the form of women. With this in mind, the Buddha said, 'In all things, there is neither male nor female.'"

Then, the goddess released her magical power and each returned to his ordinary form. She then said to him, "Reverend Sariputra, what have you done with your female form?"

Sariputra: I neither made it nor did I change it.

Goddess: Just so, all things are neither made nor changed, and that they are not made and not changed, that is the teaching of the Buddha.

VIMALAKIRTI
TRANSLATED BY ROBERT THURMAN

146

THE TREE OF LIFE

A FOLKTALE OF
TARA'S COMPASSION

In the northeast of India was a place where the monks would draw water, and at this place was an image of Tara carved on a rock. But here lived monks who practiced the Little Vehicle; and when they saw any scriptures of the Great Vehicle they took and burned them. The king was enraged when he heard that they so deeply hated the Tantra that, like enemies, they destroyed its images, and he wished to kill them. He sent men to apprehend the monks. The monks quickly knelt before the image of

Tara and begged her to save them. They suddenly heard Tara say: "Shouldn't you have sought me before you were in trouble? But I'll tell you: kneel down in the water ditch and you may yet be spared." The monks looked down the steps into the water ditch which was about the size of a bowl, and they thought, "How can we all kneel down there? It would be very difficult." Tara urged them and said, "Kneel down quickly! The guards are approaching the gate." The monks, greatly startled, crouched their bodies together and went in; and, sure enough, there was no hindrance. Thus the king looked for them, but he couldn't find them, and they were saved.

FROM AN ANCIENT COLLECTION OF "TARA" MIRACLES

CHAPTER ELEVEN

UNIVERSAL MOTHER

Hinduism

By You, this universe is borne, by You this world is created.
By You it is protected, O Devi.
By You it is consumed in the end.
You who are eternally the form of the whole world.
At the time of creation, you are the form of the creative force;
At the time of preservation you are the form of the protective power
And at the time of the dissolution of the world
You are the form of the destructive power;
You are the Supreme Knowledge, as well as ignorance,
Intellect and contemplation.

This passage from the *Devi Mahatmya*, the great Hindu hymn dedicated to the Goddess, presents an all-embracing vision of the Divine Mother, and so of the Divine Feminine. For the Hindus, everything is in the Mother, everything lives and dies in the Mother; everything is the Mother, and the Mother is everything. The entire universe is nothing but the Mother, endlessly re-creating herself out of herself, as a spider spins its web out of its own entrails and then goes to live in and along the strands it has spun out of itself.

SARASVATI, THE GODDESS OF LEARNING 12th century

India is the only country in the world where the Divine Feminine is still worshiped in many different ways and forms. Evidence of this veneration for the feminine is widely prevalent throughout India – whether revered as nature or the life force, as woman or Mother or Virgin, as Great Goddess, or as any one of her lesser emanations such as Sarasvati, Goddess of Learning, or Lakshmi, Goddess of Prosperity, or even as the supreme, ultimate, attributeless reality.

For millennia, India herself – her earth, rivers, vast fertile plains, and heart-ennobling chains of mountains – has been worshiped as a living representation of the Divine Feminine, as a Mother whose embraces extended to every kind of person and all faiths. In an ancient myth, found in the Tantras and Puranas, the God Siva became inconsolable at the death of his wife Sati, and wandered the earth in a mad dance with Sati's dead body on his shoulder. Vishnu followed him and cut up Sati's body piece by piece to relieve Siva's burden. Where fragments of her body fell to earth, fifty-two *pithas* – or pilgrimage centers – sprang up. Her *yoni* fell in Kamakhya in Assam and her right foot on the site that later became the great Mother temple, the Kalighat, in Calcutta; the whole of the Indian subcontinent, in fact, became the receptacle of her body, wholly sanctified by its contact with her.

The tradition of venerating the Divine Feminine and worshiping explicitly and exuberantly the Mother-aspect of God is very ancient in India; it dates to the Harappan culture of 3000 B.C. and earlier. Archeologists believe that mother-goddess and fertility cults in which female divinities predominated made up the most powerful part of the religious beliefs of the prehistoric period. From Kashmir, through the Vindhyan range and down into southern India, monuments that date from as early as 8000 B.C. symbolize the force of the Divine Feminine, the Shakti, "the great active female principle in the universe." All over India you find megalithic domes and dolmens built as "wombs." All over India, too, cave sanctuaries are associated with Mother Earth. The Sanskrit for "sanctuary" – and for the inmost part of any temple where the divine is encountered directly – is *garbha-gra*, "womb-chamber."

The goddess figurines found in Mohenjodaro and Harappa and the pre-Vedic "Atharva Veda" show that pre-Vedic and pre-Aryan religion in India was overwhelmingly female-centered. One Vedic female deity who, scholars believe, certainly has her roots in the pre-Vedic past, is Aditi, regarded by the Vedic seers as the Great Womb into which the entire universe has entered as "the progenitrix of cosmic creation." In the Rig Veda, Aditi is represented as containing Agni, the God of Fire and Creation, in her womb like a mother; she is the *yoni* of the universe, and most of the major Vedic gods owe their birth to her. Other goddesses celebrated in the Vedas that may well derive from earlier models include Usas, the Goddess of Dawn; Sri (Lakshmi), honored by the Devi Sukta hymn of the Rig Veda; Prithivi, Goddess of Earth; and Vac, the great Goddess of Speech and Learning.

The Vedic vision, however, and that of the Upanishads that followed them, was largely patriarchal, and the pre-Vedic goddesses to some extent went underground. It was in classical and medieval Hinduism that they were to regain their former luster and importance. It was during this period – about A.D. 400 – that the greatest hymn of all to the Goddess – the *Devi Mahatmya* – was composed. In it we find synthesized and tremendously enriched and expanded all previous Indian visions of the Divine Feminine, with a holy passion that was to influence the whole future development of Hinduism.

This immense, glorious vision of the Mother is essential to the world now because it preserves all aspects of the Mother of God in perfect mystic balance. The Mother is known at once as the transcendent source of all things, as the "Rajarajeshvari," the Supreme Sovereign Empress, who, the Hindu scriptures inform us, manifests all the dimensions of space and time out of "a fraction of a fraction" of her majesty and is also totally immanent in her own creation, in every cat, mouse, fern, and stone, in the tiniest ladybug as much as in the wild glory of the Andromeda nebula. The Mother is simultaneously infinitely beyond this or any other creation, the Creator, Preserver, and Destroyer of any creation she chooses to make out of herself,

KALI ON SIVA 18th century

and every single thing in the creation, the "good" as well as the "evil," the despised as well as the noble, the tiny as well as the gigantic. In understanding this transcendent and immanent presence of the Motherhood of God, the Hindu imagination protects all lovers of the Divine Feminine from the two main temptations that have dogged our human awareness of her – the temptation to make her purely transcendent and the temptation to make her purely immanent. If the Mother is imagined purely as a transcendent force, then she is knowable only as pure spirit or as "emptiness" and only through severe denial of life, of the body, of sexuality (which has been the patriarchal way), if the Mother is conceived as purely immanent, as present only in the body, in sexuality, in the beauties, joys, and pleasure of this life, then her whole transcendental dimension with its enormous powers of vision, illumination, and strength are ignored or simply abandoned (and this is the sad position of many contemporary feminists).

What is needed, then, is what the Hindu sacred imagination offers us – a vision of the Mother as supremely transcendent and omnipotent, but also fully, completely, consciously present in every single atom. For the Hindus, the greatness of her transcendence lies in the paradox of her ability to be present in and as every single living thing. Knowing this, realizing this, allows the child of the Mother to live, as she does, in every dimension, at once – in formless transcendent light as happily as in the body, in time with the serenity of eternity, in darkness with the knowledge of light, in the storms and terrors of history with the strong calm of infinity underlying and nourishing every thought and every action. This is perhaps the most complete vision ever given humankind of the divinity of human life, and one desperately needed now. If we are to reclaim the Divine Feminine in all its power, then we must imagine it as completely as possible.

Helping us to imagine the almost unimaginable power of the Divine Mother is one of the greatest gifts to us from the Hindu tradition and its myths and rituals. Such imagination is not an academic exercise; at this terrible moment of history, our last hope lies in a restoration of the Divine Feminine in its full force.

Only when we begin to understand how vast the Mother is will we begin to understand how powerful she is, and how powerful we, her divine children, can be, when surrendered to her, guided by her, infused with her immense, passionate, and transfiguring sacred force.

The great Mother-epic, the *Devi Mahatmya*, helps us here. In it, the Great Goddess (known in the poem by her name of Durga) is born from the combined energies of all the male divinities after they have admitted their impotence in the face of continual onslaught by their enemies, the Asuras. All the male gods' energies unite in one cosmic supernova of divine fire, and that fire, pervading the three worlds with its light, coalesces into one and becomes her. This new force, the stupendous power of the Divine Feminine, now goes into war against the Asuras – those demonic beings who, through ego-pride and greed, threaten the balance of the universe. The worlds shake and the seas tremble as Durga engages the demon Mahisasura and his hosts in the fiercest imaginable battle, creating her own female battalions from the sighs that are breathed out during the fighting. When Mahisasura, who changes shape again and again, is finally killed in his persona of buffalo-demon, the gods all praise Mother Durga, worshiping her with flowers, incense, and fragrant sandalwood paste, singing:

> *You Ambika [a name of Durga] overspread the*
> *entire universe with Your Power*
> *The power of all divine beings is drawn into Your form*
> *You are the Great Mother, worshiped by all great beings*
> *And all divine beings and all sages*
>
> *We bow ourselves in devotion to You...*
>
> *O Candika, none can speak of Your power and might,*
> *Not even Brahma, Vishnu, Siva, and Ananta.*
> *Send us Your Thoughts for the protection of the universe*
> *And for the uprooting of all dangers*
> *You whose nature it is to subdue the wicked*
> *Whose glorious loveliness is unimaginable*
> *Whose power destroys those who made the Gods powerless*
>
> *With your beautiful forms in the Three Worlds*
> *And with your terrible ones*
> *Save us in all of them.'*

The last three lines of the gods' praise to the Mother give us another clue as to the vastness and all-comprehensive nature of the Indian imagination of the Divine Feminine. Not only Durga's beautiful forms but also her terrible ones are celebrated.

The Mother is loved in India not only as the creator and preserver of the universe and of all things, but also as their destroyer.

The figure – or representation – of the Divine Mother in which this nondual embrace of the dark as well as the light aspect of creation can be most clearly seen is Kali-Kali, the "black" Mother, who makes her first appearance in the *Devi Mahatmya* as one of the formidable fighting creations of Durga, but very soon Kali becomes the entire Divine Mother in her own right. It is the black Mother Kali that India's two greatest mystics of the Mother – Ramprasad and Ramakrishna – worship as the eternal reality.

In their fearless adoration of the Mother as destroyer as well as creator, Ramprasad and Ramakrishna offer us the most glorious possible antidote to any sentimental visions we may have or want to have of the Divine Feminine. Seeing the Mother as purely tender or benign cuts us off from her (and our own) full being, as much as imagining her as either purely transcendent or purely immanent. The Mother is death, terror, horror, agony, hurricane, disaster as well as every marvelous and kind power. Learning how to adore her in her terrible as well as her benign aspect is the only way, according to both Ramprasad and Ramakrishna, of entering her total bliss, serenity, and power. How can we be one with the universe that is Her, if we reject suffering, ordeal, and death itself? How can we ever find the supreme secrets that are hidden in suffering, ordeal, and death if we do not enter their darkness with faith and profound loving trust? The great bliss and joy – her bliss and joy – that Ramprasad and Ramakrishna are trying to birth in us are unshakable and absolute precisely because they embrace all aspects of the Mother and so of the universe and life; they refuse contemptuously to identify only with those aspects of being that keep the ego happy. The bliss and joy into which they pray to birth us is as nondual as the Mother is. The divine child of the Mother, they tell us, sings through disaster as well as success, devastation as well as revelation, agony as well as peace. Knowing the Mother's laws of transformatory paradox, Ramprasad and Ramakrishna assure us, helps us turn terror into love, disaster into grace, nightmare into the shattering of illusion that prefigures the dawn of liberation; it takes us, in fact, right into the heart of the paradox of life itself and helps us birth that bliss of nondual acceptance that is the Mother's essence and her gift of freedom to anyone brave enough to consent to being torn apart by her and in her. Ramprasad wrote:

> *ll creation is the sport of my mad Mother Kali*
> *By Her maya the three worlds are bewitched*
> *Mad is She and mad is Her husband*
> *None can describe Her loveliness, Her glories, gestures, moods;*
> *Shiva, with the agony of the poison in his throat,*
> *Chants Her name again and again.*

✳

GREAT Goddess, who art thou?

She replies: I am essentially Brahman
[the Absolute.]
From me has proceeded the world
comprising Prakriti [material substance]
and Purusha [cosmic consciousness],
the void and the Plenum.

I am [all forms of] bliss and nonbliss.
Knowledge and ignorance are Myself.
I am the five elements and also what is
different from them,
the panchabhutas [five gross elements]
and tanmatras [five subtle elements].

I am the entire world.
I am the Veda as well as what is
different from it.
I am unknown.
Below and above and around am I.

FROM THE *Devi Upanishad*

She is Light itself and transcendent.
Emanating from Her body are rays
in thousands — two thousands,
a hundred thousand, tens of millions, a
hundred million — there is no counting their
numbers.

It is by and through Her that all things
moving and motionless shine.
It is by the light of this Devi that all
things become manifest.

BHAIRAVA YAMALA

A MAN once saw the image of the
Divine Mother wearing a sacred
thread. He said to the worshiper:
"What? You have put the sacred thread
on the Mother's neck!" The worshiper
said: "Brother, I see that you have truly
known the Mother. But I have not yet
been able to find out whether She is
male or female; that is why I have put
the sacred thread on Her image."

"That which is Sakti is also
Brahman. That which has form, again,
is without form. That which has
attributes, again, has no attributes.
Brahman is Sakti; Sakti is Brahman.
They are not two. They are only two
aspects, male and female, of the same
Reality, Existence-Knowledge-Bliss
Absolute."

RAMAKRISHNA
FROM *The Gospel of Ramakrishna*

WHO CAN KEEP A BLAZING FIRE TIED IN A COTTON CLOTH?

My intimate companion,
why not plunge into union
with the Great Goddess Kali?
Discover your spiritual anxiety
to be without the slightest ground.

The obscure night of your religious quest
is over and the day of truth is dawning.
The sunlight of Mother Wisdom instantly
pervades the landscape of awareness,
for darkness is not a substance
that offers resistance.
Precious Kali, you have risen as the
morning sun,
opening the lotus centers of my
subtle perception to your naked,
timeless radiance.

Proliferating systems of ritual and
philosophy attempt to throw dust
into the eyes
of the eternal wisdom that abides
in every soul.
How can any system transcend the
play of relativity?
But when relative existence is revealed
as the country fair of Mother's
sheer delight,
there are no teachers and nothing to teach,
no students and nothing to learn.

The actors and their lines are simply
expressions of the Wisdom Goddess
who directs this entire drama.
Be confident that you will soon awaken
fully as the essence of her reality!

The courageous lover tastes the bliss of the
Beloved and enters the secret city
of the Goddess,
passing beyond the threshold of ecstasy
into the open expanse of enlightenment.
Astonished by this sudden journey,
Mother's poet now sings madly:
"My delusion is gone, gone, utterly gone!
Who can obscure truth?
Who can keep a blazing fire tied
in a cotton cloth?"

FROM *Mother of the Universe:*
Poems by Ramprasad
BY LEX HIXON

T HE Primordial Power is ever at play.
She is creating, preserving and
destroying in play, as it were. This power
is called Kali. Kali is...Brahman and
Brahman is...Kali. It is one and the same
Reality. When we think of It as inactive,
that is to say, not engaged in the acts of
creation, preservation, and destruction,
then we call it Brahman. But when It
engages in these activities, then we call
it Kali or Shakti.

RAMAKRISHNA
FROM *The Gospel of Ramakrishna*

WHAT DO THEY CARE FOR THE OPINION OF THE WORLD?

The most exalted experience of bliss
*   in any realm of being*
is directly knowing the
*   universal Mother,*
the supremely blissful one.
Ecstatic lovers of Kali the Sublime
*   are not pilgrims to sacred shrines,*
for they hear all existence
*   singing the glory of the Goddess.*

These lovers of living truth
*   follow no schedule of worship*
*   or meditation*
They have lost their limited wills
*   in the limitless will of Mother,*
perceiving her alone as acting
*   through all action.*

Those who have made Kali's feet of
*   infinite delight the goal and*
*   meaning of their life*
spontaneously forget every craving
*   for egocentric power and pleasure.*
These beings of pure love sail effortlessly
across the heavy seas of birth and death,
for they are in constant contact only
*   with the root and essence of reality.*

Mother's poet sings in rapture:
"what do they care for the opinion
*   of the world?*
These lovers, eyes half-closed with
*   inward gaze,*
are drinking night and day
the sweet and powerful nectar,
Mother! Mother! Mother!"

FROM *Mother of the Universe:*
Poems by Ramprasad
BY LEX HIXON

I AM the Queen, source of thought,
    knowledge itself!
You do not know Me, yet
    you dwell in Me.
I announce Myself in words both
    gods and humans welcome.
From the summit of the world,
    I give birth to the sky!
The tempest is My breath, all living
    creatures are My life!
Beyond the wide earth,
    beyond the vast heaven,
My grandeur extends forever!

FROM THE *Devi Sukta*

I am the intelligence from which the universe emanates and in which it inheres, like a reflection in a mirror. The ignorant believe I am merely inert matter, but the wise experience me as the true Self within themselves. They glimpse me when their minds become as still and clear as an ocean without waves.

Brahma, Vishnu, Shiva, the gods of all the directions and their energies, indeed every entity on all planes of existence, are manifestations of myself. My power is too vast to be imagined. Yet beings do not know me because their minds are shrouded in ignorance. That too is my power.

The supreme wisdom is that which ends the delusion that anyone or anything exists apart from myself. The fruit of this realization is fearlessness and the end of sorrow. When one realizes that all the limitless universes are a fraction of an atom in the unity of my being, that all the numberless lives in the universes are a wisp of vapor in one of my breaths, that all the triumphs and tragedies, the good and evil in all the worlds, are merely my unconsidered, spontaneous play, then life and death stand still, and the drama of individual life evaporates like a shallow pond on a warm day.

You are experiencing me now, yet you do not recognize me. There is no remedy for your ignorance other than to worship me as your innermost Self. Surrender yourself to me with joyful one-pointed devotion, and I will help you discover your true being. Abide in consciousness as continuously and effortlessly as the ignorant abide in their bodies. Abide in me as I abide in you. Know that even now, there is absolutely no difference between us. Realize it now!"

FROM THE *Tipura Rahasya Tantra*

WHATEVER we see or think about is the manifestation of the Mother, of the Primordial Energy, the Primal Consciousness. Creation, preservation, and destruction, living beings and the universe, and further, meditation and the meditator, bhakti [devotion] and prema [divine love] — all these are manifestations of the glory of that Power...

Brahman, the Godhead, and Shakti, the Primal Energy, are like the snake and its wriggling motion. Thinking of the snake, one must think of its wriggling motion, and thinking of the wriggling motion, one must think of the snake. Or they are like milk and its whiteness. Thinking of milk one has to think of its color, that is, whiteness, and thinking of the whiteness of milk, one has to think of milk itself. Or they are like water and its wetness. Thinking of water one has to think of its wetness, and thinking of the wetness of water, one has to think of water...

RAMAKRISHNA
FROM *The Gospel of Ramakrishna*

I HAVE RAISED BOTH MY HANDS

It is a joy to merge the mind in the Indivisible Brahman through contemplation. And it is also a joy to keep the mind on the Lila, the Relative, without dissolving it in the Absolute.

A mere jnani is a monotonous person. He always analyzes, saying: "It is not this, not this. The world is like a dream." But I have "raised both my hands." Therefore I accept everything.

Listen to a story. Once a woman went to see her weaver friend. The weaver, who had been spinning different kinds of silk thread, was very happy to see her friend and said to her: "Friend, I can't tell you how happy I am to see you. Let me get you some refreshment." She left the room. The woman looked at the threads of different colors and was tempted.

She hid a bundle of thread under one arm. The weaver returned presently with the refreshments and began to feed her guest with enthusiasm. But, looking at the thread, she realized that her friend had taken a bundle. Hitting upon a plan to get it back, she said: "Friend, it is so long since I have seen you. This is a day of great joy for me. I feel very much like asking you to dance with me." The friend said, "Sister, I am feeling very happy too." So the two friends began to dance together. When the weaver saw that her friend danced without raising her hands, she said: "Friend, let us dance with both hands raised. This is a day of great joy." But the guest pressed one arm to her side and danced raising only the other. The weaver said: "How is this, friend? Why should you dance with only one hand raised? Dance with me raising both hands. Look at me. See how I dance with both hands raised." But the guest still pressed one arm to her side. She danced with the other hand raised and said with a smile, "This is all I know of dancing."

The Master continued: "I don't press my arm to my side. Both my hands are free. I am not afraid of anything. I accept both the Nitya and the Lila, both the Absolute and the Relative."

RAMAKRISHNA
FROM *The Gospel of Ramakrishna*

HYMN TO DURGA

THAT power who is defined as
  Consciousness in all beings,
reverence to Her, reverence to Her,
  reverence to Her,
reverence, reverence.

That power who is known as Reason
  in all being,
reverence to Her, reverence to Her,
  reverence to Her,
reverence, reverence.

That power who exists in all beings in
  the form of Sleep,
reverence to Her, reverence to Her,
  reverence to Her,
reverence, reverence.

That power who exists
  in all beings as Hunger,
reverence to Her, reverence to Her,
  reverence to Her,
reverence, reverence.

That power who exists
  in all beings as Shadow,
reverence to Her, reverence to Her,
  reverence to Her,
reverence, reverence.

FROM THE *Devi Mahatmya*

THE MOTHER

*The Divine Mother revealed to me in the
Kali temple that it was She who had
become everything. She showed me that
everything was full of Consciousness. The
Image was Consciousness, the altar was
Consciousness, the water-vessels were
Consciousness, the door-sill was
Consciousness, the marble floor was
Consciousness – all was Consciousness.*

*I found everything inside the room soaked,
as it were, in Bliss – the Bliss of
Satchidananda. I saw a wicked man in front
of the Kali temple; but in him also I saw
the Power of the Divine Mother vibrating.*

*That was why I fed a cat with the food that
was to be offered to the Divine Mother.
I clearly perceived that the Divine Mother
Herself had become everything –
even the cat.*

RAMAKRISHNA
FROM *The Gospel of Ramakrishna*

CHAPTER TWELVE

MOTHER TO ALL CREATION

Taoism

The Tao is the breath that never dies.
It is a Mother to All Creation.

TAO TE CHING 6
FROM *Tao Te Ching*
BY MAN-HO KWOK, MARTIN PALMER, JAY RAMSAY

*O*nce, in China, as elsewhere, there was a Mother who *was* before heaven and earth came into being. Her image was woven into the age-old beliefs of the people and the shamanic tradition that later evolved into Taoism. In Chinese mythology the Mother Goddess has many names and titles. One legend imagined her as an immense peach tree that grew in the Garden of Paradise and was the support of the whole universe. The fruit of this marvelous and magical tree ripened only after three thousand years, bestowing immortality on whoever tasted it. The Garden of Paradise belonged to the Queen of the Immortals, whose name was Hsi Wang Mu, Goddess of Eternal Life. Other myths describe her as the Mother or Grandmother, the primordial heavenly being, the cosmic womb of all life, the gateway of heaven and earth. Taoism developed on this foundation.

THE TAOIST GODDESS KUAN YIN

KUAN YIN, GODDESS OF COMPASSION

More subtly and comprehensively than any other religious tradition, Taoism nurtured the quintessence of the Divine Feminine, keeping alive the feeling of relationship with the ground of being as Primordial Mother. Somehow the Taoist sages discovered how to develop the mind without losing touch with the soul.

The origins of Taoism come from the shamanic practices and oral traditions of the Bronze Age and beyond. Its earliest written expression is the *Book of Changes* or *I Ching*, a book of divination consisting of sixty-four oracles, which is thought to date to 3000–1200 B.C. The complementary images of yin and yang woven into the sixty-four hexagrams of the *I Ching* are not to be understood as two separate expressions of the one indivisible life energy – earth and heaven, feminine and masculine, female and male – for each contains elements of the other and each cannot exist without the other. In their passionate embrace, there is relationship, dialogue, and continual movement and change. The *I Ching* describes the flow of energies of the Tao in relation to a particular time, place, or situation and helps the individual to balance the energies of yin and yang and to listen to the deeper resonance of the One that is both.

The elusive essence of Taoism is expressed in the *Tao Te Ching*, the only work of the great sage Lao Tzu (born c. 604 B.C.), whom legend says was persuaded by one of his disciples to write down the eighty-one sayings. The word *Tao* means the fathomless Source, the One, the Deep. *Te* is the way the Tao comes into being, growing organically like a plant from the deep ground or source of life, from within outward. *Ching* is the slow, patient shaping of that growth through the activity of a creative intelligence that is expressed as the organic patterning of all instinctual life, like the DNA of the universe. "The Tao does nothing, yet nothing is left undone." The tradition of Taoism was transmitted from master to pupil by a succession of shaman-sages, many of whom were sublime artists and poets. In the midst of the turmoil of the dynastic struggles that engulfed China for centuries they followed the Tao, bringing together the outer world of appearances with the inner one of being.

From the source that is both everything and nothing, and whose image is the circle, came heaven and earth, yin and yang – the two principles whose dynamic relationship brings into being the world we see. The Tao is both the source and the creative process of life that flows from it, imagined as a Mother who is the root of heaven and earth, beyond all yet within all, giving birth to all, containing all, nurturing all. The Way of Tao is to reconnect with the mother source or ground, to be in it, like a bird in the air or a fish in the sea, in touch with it, while living in the midst of what the Taoists called the "sons" or "children" – the myriad forms that the source takes in manifestation. It is to become aware of the presence of the Tao in everything, to discover its rhythm and its dance, to learn to trust it, no longer interfering with the flow of life by manipulating, directing, resisting, controlling. It is to develop the intuitive awareness of a mystery that only gradually reveals itself. Following the Way of Tao requires a turning toward the hidden withinness of things, a receptivity to instinctive feeling, and enough time to reflect on what is inconceivable and indescribable, beyond the reach of mind or intellect. Action taken from this position of balance and freedom will gradually become aligned to the harmony of the Tao and will therefore embody its mysterious power and wisdom.

The Taoists never separated nature from spirit, consciously preserving the instinctive knowledge that life is one. No people observed nature more passionately and minutely than the Chinese sages, or reached so deeply into the hidden heart of life, describing the life and form of insects, animals, birds, flowers, trees, wind, water, planets, and stars. They felt the continuous flow and flux of life as an underlying energy that was without beginning or end, that was, like water, never static, never still, never fixed in separate things or events, but always in a state of movement, a state of changing and becoming. They called the art of going with the flow of this energy Wu Wei, not-doing (*Wu* means not or non-, *Wei* means doing, making, striving after goals). Wu Wei meant relinquishing control, not trying to force or manipulate life but attuning oneself to the underlying rhythm and ever-changing modes of its being. The stilling of the surface mind that is preoccupied with the ten thousand things brings into being a deeper, more complete mind, and an integrated state of consciousness or creative power that they named Te, which enabled them not to interfere with life but to "enter the forest without moving the grass; to enter the water without raising a ripple."

They cherished the Tao with their brushstrokes, observing how it flowed into the patterns of cloud and mist between earth and mountain peak, or the rhythms of air currents and the eddying water of rivers and streams. They listened to the sounds that can only be attended to in silence. They expressed their experience of the Tao in their paintings, their poetry, the creation of their temples and gardens, and in their way of living, which was essentially one of withdrawal from the world to a place where they could live a simple, contemplative life, concentrating on perfecting their brushstrokes in calligraphy and painting, and their subtlety of expression in the art of poetry. Humility, reverence, patience, insight, and wisdom were the qualities they sought to cultivate.

The Taoist artist or poet intuitively reached into the secret essence of what he was observing, making himself one with it, then inviting it to speak through him, so releasing the dynamic harmony within it. He imposed nothing of himself on it but reflected the creative soul of what he was observing through the highly developed skills that he had cultivated over a lifetime of practice. Through the perfection of his art, he did not define or explain the Tao, which, as Chuang-Tzu said, cannot be conveyed either by words or by silence, but called it into focus so that it could be experienced by the beholder. The Tao flows through the whole work as cosmic presence, at once transcendent in its mystery and immanent in its form. The distillation of what the Taoist sages discovered is bequeathed to us in the beauty and wisdom of their painting and poetry, and in their profound understanding of the relationship between body, soul, and nature, and the eternal ground that underlies and enfolds them all.

Standing before one of the great Taoist paintings of the T'ang or Sung dynasties or reading a poem by Wang Wei, one is immediately transformed by them, able to let go of the things that normally distract the mind and exhaust the body – the preoccupation with the ten thousand things that the Taoists called "dust." They put one in touch with the center simply by relating one instantaneously to the ground which unifies everything.

To rest in the quietness of mind and humility of heart, which the Taoist sage embodies, is to live in a state of instinctive spontaneity that the Taoists named Tzu Jan

STATUE OF THE
BODHISATTVA KUAN YIN

– a being-in-the-moment that can only exist, as in childhood, when the effort to adapt to collective values and the need to accumulate possessions, power, or fame is of no importance. What exists is what is. There is no need to change it by imposing the will. Change will come about by changing the quality of one's own being. To feel what needs to be said without striving to say it; to speak from the heart in as few words as possible; to act when action is required, responding to the needs of the moment without attachment to the fruits of action, this is the essence of the Taoist vision. It is essentially feminine, gentle, balanced, dynamic, and wise.

The image of the primordial Mother was embedded deep within the soul of the Chinese people who, as in Egypt, Sumer, and India, turned to her for help and support in time of need. She was particularly close to women who prayed to her for the blessing of children, for a safe delivery in childbirth, for the protection of their families, for the healing of sickness. Their Mother Goddess was not a remote being but a compassionate, accessible presence in their homes, in the sacred mountains where they went on pilgrimages to her temples and shrines, and in the valleys and vast forests where she could be felt, and sometimes seen. Yet, like the goddesses in other early cultures, she also had cosmic dimensions. Guardian of the waters, helper of the souls of the dead in their passage to other realms, she was the Great Mother who responded to the cry of all people who called upon her in distress. She was the spirit of life itself, caring for suffering humanity, her child. Above all, she was the embodiment of mercy, love, compassion, and wisdom, the protectress of life. Although she had many names and images in earlier times, these eventually merged into one goddess who was called Kuan Yin – she who hears, she who listens.

By a fascinating process that saw the blending of different religious traditions, the ancient Chinese Mother Goddess absorbed elements of the Buddhist image of the bodhisattva Avalokitesvara, the Tibetan Mother Goddess Tara, and the Virgin Mary of Christianity, whose statues were brought to China during the seventh century A.D. The name Kuan Yin was a translation of the sanskrit word *Avalokitesvara* and means "The One Who Hears the Cries of the World." At first, following the Mahayana Buddhist tradition, this compassionate being was imagined in male form, but from the fifth century A.D., the female form of Kuan Yin begins to appear in China, and by the tenth century it predominated.

It was in the far northwest, at the interface between Chinese, Tibetan, and European civilizations, that the cult of Kuan Yin took strongest root, and it was from here that it spread throughout China and into Korea and Japan (where her name was Kannon), grafted onto the far older image of the Mother Goddess. Every province had its local image and its own story about her. Taoist and Buddhist elements were fused, creating an image of the Divine Feminine that was deeply satisfying to the people. By the sixteenth century, Kuan Yin had become the principal deity of China and Japan and is so today. Robed in white, she is usually shown seated or standing on a lotus throne, sometimes with a child on her lap or near her, for she brings the blessing of children to women.

Chinese Buddhist texts describe her as being within a vast circle of light that emanates from her body, her face gleaming golden, surrounded with a garland of 8,000 rays. The palms of her hands radiate the color of 500 lotus flowers. The tip of each finger has 84,000 images, each emitting 84,000 rays whose gentle radiance touches all things. All beings are drawn to her and compassionately embraced by her. Meditation on this image is said to free them from the endless cycle of birth and death.

THE Tao that can be told is not
the eternal Tao.
The name that can be named is not
the eternal Name.
The nameless is the beginning of
heaven and earth.
The named is the mother of ten
thousand things.
Ever desireless, one can see the mystery.
Ever desiring, one can see the
manifestations.
These two spring from the same source
but differ in name;
this appears as darkness.
Darkness within darkness.
The gate to all mystery.

TAO TE CHING 1
FROM *Tao Te Ching*
BY GIA FU-FENG AND JANE ENGLISH

*There was something formless
yet complete,
That existed before heaven and earth;
Without sound, without substance,
Dependent on nothing, unchanging,
all pervading, unfailing.
One may think of it as the mother of
all things under heaven.
Its true name we do not know.*

TAO TE CHING 25
FROM *The Way and its Power*
BY ARTHUR WALEY

STORE the spirit and energy away
in mystical darkness, and the bit of
spiritual root will grow from faintness
to clarity, from softness to strength.
When the process is complete,
suddenly you will break through space
to reveal the pure spiritual body,
leaping beyond the worlds. This is
like when the caterpillar, having
transformed into a moth, breaks out of
its cocoon and flies away, or like when
the polliwog becomes a frog and leaps.
There is a body beyond the body,
another world.

FROM *Awakening to the Tao*
BY LIU I-MING

*The Valley Spirit never dies.
It is named the Mysterious Female
And the Doorway of the
Mysterious Female
Is the base from which Heaven
and Earth sprang.
It is there within us all the while;
Draw upon it as you will,
it never runs dry.*

TAO TE CHING 6
FROM *The Way and its Power*
BY ARTHUR WALEY

172

WHEN the moon rises in the
    Heart of Heaven
and a light breeze touches the
    mirror-like face of the lake.
That indeed is a moment of pure joy.
But few are they who are aware of it.

ANONYMOUS
FROM Creativity and Taoism
BY CHANG CHUNG-YUAN

Concentrate on the goal of meditation.
Do not listen with your ear but listen
    with your mind;
Not with your mind but with your breath.
Let hearing stop with your ear,
Let the mind stop with its images.
Breathing means to empty oneself and
    to wait for Tao.
Tao abides only in the emptiness.
This emptiness is the fasting mind…
Look at the Void! In its chamber
    light is produced.
Lo! Joy is here to stay.

CHUANG TZU
FROM Creativity and Taoism
BY CHANG CHUNG-YUAN

THAT which you look at but cannot
    see
Is called the Invisible.
That which you listen to but cannot
    hear
Is called the Inaudible.
That which you grasp but cannot hold
Is called the Unfathomable.

None of these three can be inquired
    after,
Hence they blend into one.
Above no light can make it lighter,
Beneath no darkness can make it
    darker.

Unceasingly it continues
But it is impossible to define.
Again it returns to nothingness
Thus it is described as the Form
    of the Formless,
The Image of the Imageless.
Hence it is called the Evasive.

It is met with but no one sees its face;
It is followed but no one sees its back.
To hold the Tao of old,
To deal with the affairs at hand,
In order to understand the primordial
    beginnings,
That is called the rule of Tao.

TAO TE CHING 14
FROM Creativity and Taoism
BY CHANG CHUNG-YUAN

THE GODDESS AMATERASU EMERGING FROM
THE EARTH
Utagawa Kunisada 1786–1865

Push far enough towards the Void,
Hold fast enough to Quietness,
And of the ten thousand things
none but can be worked on by you.
I have beheld them, whither they go back.
See, all things howsoever they flourish
Return to the root from which they grew.
This return to the Root is called Quietness;
Quietness is called submission to Fate;
What has submitted to Fate has become
*   part of the always-so;*
To know the always-so is to be Illumined;
Not to know it, means to go
*   blindly to disaster.*
He who know the always-so has room in
*   him for everything;*
He who has room in him for everything
*   is without prejudice.*
To be without prejudice is to be kingly;
To be kingly is to be of heaven;
To be of heaven is to be in Tao.
Tao is forever and he that possesses it,
Though his body ceases, is not destroyed.

TAO TE CHING 16
FROM *The Way and its Power*
BY ARTHUR WALEY

IN manifesting the world,
    Tao becomes the Universal Mother.
In the knowledge of the Mother is the
    knowledge of her children.
And this childhood being known,
    there is access to the Mother.
Thus, life is unaffected though body
    fade away.
He who closes his lips and shuts the
    doors of his senses,
    all his life is free from turmoil.
He who opens his mouth and spends
    his breath in vain pursuits,
    all his life cannot his safety keep.
In the perception of the smallest is the
    secret of clear vision;
In the guarding of the weakest is the
    secret of all strength.
He who neglects the Inner Light is lost
    in body's darkness.
He who follows the Light of Heaven
    ever reflects its radiance.
This is called the Eternal Heritage.

TAO TE CHING 52
FROM *The Shrine of Wisdom*

FLOWERING HILLS IN SPRING *Lan Ying* 1585–1664

Since the days of my middle life
I was deeply devoted to Tao.
Recently I came to live
In the mountains of Chung-nan.
Oftentimes – with joy in my heart –
Alone, I roam here and there.
It is a wonderful thing
That I am aware of myself.
When the streamlet ends my trip
I settle down and catch the moment
of rising mists.
Now and then I meet
A furrowed dweller of the woods.
We chat and laugh; Never do I want
to go home.

WANG WEI
FROM *Creativity and Taosim*
BY CHANG CHUNG-YUAN

WE can hold back neither
the coming of the flowers
nor the downward rush of the stream;
sooner or later, everything comes
to its fruition.

The rhythms are called by the
Great Mother,
the Heavenly Father.
All the rest is but a dream;
We need not disturb our sleeping.

FROM *The Book of the Heart*
BY LOY CHING-YUEN

The Way is like an empty vessel
That yet may be drawn from
without ever needing to be filled.
It is bottomless; the very progenitor
of all things in the world.
In it all sharpness is blunted,
All tangles untied,
All glare tempered,
All dust smoothed.
It is like a deep pool that never dries...

TAO TE CHING 4
FROM *The Way and its Power*
BY ARTHUR WALEY

THE TAO is priceless, a pearl
containing Creation. In storage, it is
utterly dark, without a trace. Brought
out, its light shines through day and
night. Becoming wise depends entirely
on this – you need nothing else to be
enlightened. So many Taoists seek at
random, all the while casting aside the
treasure at hand.

FROM *Awakening to the Tao*
BY LIU I-MING

The wide pond expands
   like a mirror,
The heavenly light and cloud shadows
   play upon it.
How does such clarity occur?
It is because it contains the living
   stream from the Fountain.

CHU HSI
FROM *Creativity and Taoism*
BY CHANG CHUNG-YUAN

HE who knows the male,
   yet cleaves to what is female
Becomes like a ravine, receiving
   all things under heaven
And being such a ravine
he knows all the time a power that he
   never calls upon in vain.

TAO TE CHING 28
FROM *The Way and its Power*
BY ARTHUR WALEY

Out of non-being, being is born;
Out of silence, the writer produces a song.

LU CHI
FROM *Wen Fu: The Art of Writing*
TRANSLATED BY SAM HAMILL

THE ancient masters were subtle,
   mysterious, profound, responsive.
The depth of their knowledge
   is unfathomable.
Because it is unfathomable,
All we can do is describe
   their appearance.
Watchful, like men crossing a
   winter stream.
Alert, like men aware of danger.
Courteous, like visiting guests.
Yielding, like ice about to melt.
Simple, like uncarved blocks
   of wood.
Hollow, like caves.
Opaque, like muddy pools.

Who can wait quietly while
   the mud settles?
Who can remain still until the
   moment of action?
Observers of the Tao do not seek
   fulfillment.
Not seeking fulfillment, they are not
   swayed by desire for change.

TAO TE CHING 15
FROM Tao Te Ching
BY GIA FU-FENG AND JANE ENGLISH

POEM TO KUAN YIN

Her knowledge fills out
   the four virtues,
Her wisdom suffuses her golden body.
Her necklace is hung with pearls and
   precious jade,
Her bracelet is composed of jewels.
Her hair is like dark clouds wondrously
   arranged like curling dragons;
Her embroidered girdle sways like a
   phoenix's wing in flight.
Sea-green jade buttons,
A gown of pure silk,
Awash with Heavenly light;
Eyebrows as if crescent moons,
Eyes like stars.
A radiant jade face of divine joyfulness,
Scarlet lips, a splash of color.
Her bottle of heavenly dew overflows,
Her willow twig rises from it
   in full flower.
She delivers from all the eight terrors,
Saves all living beings,
For boundless is her compassion.
She resides on T'ai Shan,
She dwells in the Southern Ocean.
She saves all the suffering when their
   cries reach her,
She never fails to answer their prayers,
Eternally divine and wonderful.

FROM *Kuan Yin*
BY MARTIN PALMER, JAY RAMSAY, AND MAN-HO KWOK

*L*isten to the deeds of Kuan Yin
Responding compassionately on every side
With great vows, deep as the ocean,
Through inconceivable periods of time,
Serving innumerable Buddhas,
Giving great, clear, and pure vows...
To hear her name, to see her body,
To hold her in the heart, is not in vain,
For she can extinguish the suffering
   of existence.

FROM THE *Buddhist Lotus Sutra*

In the deep bamboo forest I sit alone.
Loudly I sing and tune my lute.
The forest is so thick that no one
   knows about it.
Only the bright moon comes to
   shine upon me.

WANG WEI
FROM *Creativity and Taoism*
BY CHANG CHUNG-YUAN

FISHING IN A MOUNTAIN STREAM
11th century

CHAPTER THIRTEEN

THE RETURN OF
THE DIVINE FEMININE

*J*ust before he died in 1950 the great Hindu mystic of the Mother, Aurobindo, is said to have remarked: "If there is to be a future it will wear the crown of female design."

Perhaps the most significant feature of the last forty years has been the recovery in every area of life of the power of the feminine and an increasingly conscious and passionate turning – visible everywhere – to the feminine aspect of God. The life of our planet is under threat; our survival as a species is uncertain. Unless we wake up to the full reality of what we have done and are doing to the planet, it may be too late to alter the course of events we have unwittingly set in motion. In response to this crisis, the Divine Feminine is activated in the depths of our soul to help us see what needs to be done and to do it.

Gathering awareness of ecological catastrophe and our alienation from nature has led to a vast intellectual, spiritual, and artistic effort to re-imagine the feminine face of God. Many people now believe that, unless the wisdom of the Divine Feminine is recognized, celebrated, and integrated with the masculine at every level and in every arena of culture, society, and politics, the human race will not be able to evolve the mystical-practical balance it needs to survive.

The "Return of the Goddess or Mother" expresses itself in myriad different ways: in a powerful feminism that draws on the various symbols of the Goddess or Mother to effect a revaluation of the role of women at every level; in many forms of psychotherapy – most notably, perhaps, Jungian – that encourage awareness of the long-derided inner world of dreams, visions, and archetypal images and symbols; in holistic scientific visions of the unity and interdependence of the cosmos such as the Gaia thesis of James Lovelock, which has heightened ecological consciousness everywhere; in widespread challenges to, and internal reforms of, all the existing religions; in a turning away from old hierarchical forms of spiritual transmission in favor of a more direct relationship with the Divine; in an increasingly subtle emphasis on kinds of therapy and body work that aim to heal the profound split between mind and body; in a return to an ancient, tolerant, Tantric vision of sacred sexuality that transforms the Judeo-Christian image of the body and sexuality as sinful. The long-denied Mother is returning in many ways and forms to guide and inspire her children in their most endangered moment and give birth to a new, healed humanity.

Increasingly, too, this recovery of the Sacred Feminine is being seen and felt as a call to worldwide political and economic change. The Divine Feminine is Love-in-Action: to connect with its vast force of compassion is inevitably to connect with a divine longing to see all earthly conditions transformed to mirror the central law of love and justice. On whether or not humanity can answer this call for transformation at every level depends our future.

OUR LADY

Lady, how can I speak,
  my mouth silent
as the hills, dumb with fear and desire?
Lady of Myriad Names, your beauty
  and destruction
freeze my heart – how can I
  approach You

from the city paved with bone?
  Highways roar
with trucks of nerve gas, rivers carry
  poisoned fish
and human heads, villages are wrecked,
  people starving,
war missiles planted throughout
  the earth.

Shall I call You Dachau? Our Lady of
  Hiroshima?
For your skies are fumed with flesh,
  Horrible
Kali, Wretched Ereshkigal,
  Suffering One!
You wove the world of dark and light,

made the ways illumined
  and unknowable,
No Lady – of appetite, of difference,
  of need.
When You move the volcano rumbles,
  hurricanes blow,

clouds burst, rain falls, rivers rush and
  earth shudders,
Lady of All That Is. Bringing life
  to emptiness,
You cooled the fiery earth –
  who boldly made orange sky,
the blinding light – and made
  the rocks where trees
and grasses, poppies, broom, and
  waving mustard grow.

Candelabras of magnolia, lavender,
  cones of lilac,
coral camelias, cascades of acacia,
  purple crocus,
yellow daffodil, pale cherry, and
  lacy alyssum!
Into air You sent the
  shimmering dragonfly,

darting hummingbird, crying quail,
  great eagle,
blue heron, and red-tailed hawk
  ever circling.
Magnificent Lady, your mouth
  is trembling,
aging, more vulnerable than before.

Behold: Swift scorpions, sweet lobsters,
  smart octopi,
shy whales, and schools of
  diving dolphin;
solitary deer roaming radiation lab in
  moonlight,

184

wide-eared elephant, crouching lion,
  and waiting dog.

You made them, Lady of Visions,
  who now destroy.
Strange machines march from
  your mighty thighs
and all of Earth is afraid —
  through atmospheric decay
brass sun shines harshly.

And through time the poets cry —
Sappho, Tu Fu, Kabir, Hoelderlin,
  Shelley.
Do You hear Emily whose heart
  pours longing —
for she saw your body naked,
  your arms rivers of light! ...
Like Emily I have been wandering
in your marshes, like the insect,
stumbling lover in the wet dark flower.

So take me, Unattainable and
  Only Lady
over your great loom and weave me
  according to design.
Guide me through chaos, and though I
  cannot find You
be with me as any creature in the field
now and always, living or dead,
on the vast arcs of energy certain and
  turbulent,
or lost tossed in your void,

Great Wombed Mother.
For You will be whether I know it
  or not.

Bring love, fertility, and warmth to
  my frozen soul
and fill heart's empty bed, though
  a small thing
in the enormity of your
  unfolding Desire —
Lady of the Universe, Kind Lady
  Kwan Yin,

Mother of God, of all the gods,
  avatars, and saints,
the childish artists who crave to
  touch your shape,
even the evil ones crushed in
  your inscrutable heart.
Wise Sophia — Shekinah —
  hear my prayer.

And when I drop my body into yours,
snuffed in the scents of your
  magnificent dream
as loss upon loss gushes from your
  unfathomable depths,
clasp me in your infinite gaze, Lady of
  All Knowledge.

JANINE CANAN
FROM *She Rises Like the Sun*
EDITED BY JANINE CANAN

CLIFF'S EDGE

As I walk the cliff's edge,
Sun throws open her cape
and Ocean flashes a million mirrors.

Unexpectedly, the Dark One enters
and shoves her gleaming blade in my heart.

Now under a million blazing stars,
I drop my name
and kneel before my pain. What shall I do?

Accept everything that I give you,
She answers.
I am everything – you are burning
with My Life.

JANINE CANAN
FROM *She Rises Like the Sun*
EDITED BY JANINE CANAN

THE SOURCE

IN the secret place of
The Most High
I nestle
Waiting for the moment
Listening for the song
That connects me to
Thee
Womb of all Being
Divine Source
Lost Shekhinah of my soul
Immortal Presence!

ANNE BARING

THE SONG

Beehive source
Trellised womb
Mother of all beginnings

Hold me
Gather me
Feed me
With the honey-nectar
From the hive.

Nourished
I will sing
The Bee-song
The long-forgotten threnody
Of praise to thee.

ANNE BARING

PREPARING TO GREET THE GODDESS

Do not think of her
unless you are prepared
to be driven to your limits,
to rush forth from yourself
like a ritual bowl overflowing
with consecrated wine.

Do not summon her image
unless you are ready to be blinded,
to stand in the flash
of a center exploding,
yourself shattering into the landscape,
wavering bits of bark and water.

Do not speak her name
until you have said goodbye
to all your familiar trinkets —
your mirrors, your bracelets,
your childhood adorations —
From now on you are nothing,
a ghost hovering at the window,
a voice singing under water.

DOROTHY WATERS

SHEKHINAH

To our desert ancestors she was the
  Divine Presence
who they carried in the sacred ark
the clouds of glory that guided them
and the manna that nourished them.
To the Talmudic sages she was the
  Divine Presence
who dwelled in the holy temple
  in Jerusalem,
the spirit that surrounds us when
  we pursue justice
and leaves when there is pollution
  and violence.

To the Medieval Pietists, she was the
  Divine Presence
who sat at the celestial throne of glory,
receiving our prayers
and radiating back the light to all beings.

To the authors of the Zohar, she was the
  Divine Presence
moving through the tree of life as Binah,
  Great Ocean Mother;
Gevurah, the Destroyer; Hod the Glory;
and Malchuth, the Earth.

To the Safat Kabbalists, she was the
  Divine Presence
as "pardes" holy apple orchard and
  Shabbos Queen,

whose reunification with the Divine King
was the goal of all prayers and
  ritual actions.

To the Hasidic Masters, she was the
  Divine Presence
who shone on the faces of righteous
  women and men,
Mother of the soul's breath
her return to earth was the goal
  of their prayers.

To our diaspora foremothers, she was the
  Divine Presence
as the compassionate source,
the one they called out to in childbirth,
  illness and death
and celebrated on the New Moon.

And to us, contemporary Jewish seekers,
she is the Divine Presence

in the voice of women, representing the
Shekhinah reawakening

who is calling to us from the earth
save the planet, stop the nuclear
  madness, clear the air
heal the sick, respect the elders,
  care for the children

and to her, we respond ...

we are ready to create a dwelling place
for the divine here on earth

to her, we answer …

in music and meditation
in politics and poetry
in dance and drama

to her we respond …
… "Hineynu" …
Yes, we are here.

RABBI LÉAH NOVICK

INVOCATION

I WHO am the beauty of the
    green earth
and the white moon among the stars,
and the mysteries of the waters,
I call upon your soul to arise and
    come unto me.
For I am the soul of nature that gives
    life to the universe.
From Me all things proceed and unto
    Me they must return.
Let my worship be in the heart
    that rejoices,
for behold — all acts of love and
    pleasure are my rituals.
Let there be beauty and strength,
    power and compassion,
honor and humility, mirth and

reverence within you.
And you who seek to know Me,
    know that your
seeking and yearning will
    avail you not, unless
you know the Mystery:
For if that which you seek, you find
    not within yourself,
you will never find it without.
For behold, I have been with
    you from the
beginning, and I am that which is
    attained at the end of desire.

POEM VERSION BY STARHAWK
ORIGINAL BY DOREEN VALIENTE

BIBLIOGRAPHY

ATOM FROM THE SUN OF KNOWLEDGE

Lex Hixon

(Shambhala Publications, Boston, Mass., 1994)

AWAKENING TO THE TAO

Liu I-Ming

(Shambhala Publications, Boston, Mass., 1988)

CREATIVITY AND TAOISM

Chang Chung-Yuan

(Wildwood House, Aldershot, Hampshire, 1975)

EGYPTIAN MYSTERIES

Lucy Lamy

(Thames and Hudson, London, 1981)

HYMNES ET PRIERES DE L'EGYPTE ANCIENNE

A. Barucq and F. Dumas

(Les Editions du Cerf, Paris, 1981)

HYMNS TO ISIS IN HER TEMPLE AT PHILAE

translated by Louis V. Zabkar

(University Press of New England, Hanover, NH, 1988)

INANNA, QUEEN OF HEAVEN AND EARTH

D. Wolkstein and S. M. Kramer

(HarperCollins, New York, 1983)

KINGSHIP AND THE GODS

H. Frankfort

(University of Chicago Press, 1976)

KUAN YIN: MYTHS AND PROPHECIES OF THE CHINESE GODDESS OF COMPASSION

Martin Palmer, Jay Ramsay, and Man-Ho Kwok

(HarperCollins, 1995)

MOTHER OF THE BUDDHAS: MEDITATIONS ON THE PRAJNAPARAMITA SUTRA

Lex Hixon

(Quest Books, Ill., 1993)

MOTHER OF THE UNIVERSE: POEMS BY RAMPRASAD

Lex Hixon

(Quest Books, Ill., 1994)

RETURN OF THE MOTHER
Andrew Harvey
(Frog Ltd, 1995)

SHE RISES LIKE THE SUN
edited by Janine Canan
(Crossing Press, 1989)

SUMERIAN AND BABYLONIAN PSALMS
Stephen Langdon
(Librairie Paul Geuther, Paris, 1909)

TAO TE CHING
Lao Tzu, translated by Gia-Fu Feng and Jane English
(Wildwood House, Aldershot, Hampshire, 1992)

TAO TE CHING
Man-Ho Kwok, Martin Palmer, and Jay Ramsay
(Element Books, Shaftesbury, Dorset, and Rockport, Mass., 1993)

THE BOOK OF THE HEART
Loy Ching-Yuen
(Shambhala Publications, Boston, Mass., 1988)

THE GOSPEL OF SRI RAMAKRISHNA
translated by Swami Nikhilananda
(Madras, India, n.d.)

THE MYTH OF THE GODDESS
Anne Baring and Jules Cashford
(Penguin, Arkana, 1992)

THE POETRY OF SUMER
S. M. Kramer
(University of California Press, Berkeley, Ca., 1979)

THE WAY AND ITS POWER
Arthur Waley
(Allen and Unwin, 1934)

TWO SUNS RISING
Jonathan Star
(Bantam Books, 1991)

WOMEN IN PRAISE OF THE SACRED
by Jane Hirshfield
(HarperCollins, New York, 1979)

ACKNOWLEDGMENTS

The publishers would like to thank the following sources for permission to reproduce copyright material. Every effort has been made to contact copyright holders and the publishers would like to apologise for any inadvertent errors and will be pleased to correct these in subsequent editions.

George Allen and Unwin: Excerpts from THE WAY AND ITS POWER by Arthur Waley. Copyright © 1934 Arthur Waley.

E. J. Brill: Excerpts from THE NAG HAMMADI LIBRARY (ed. James M. Robinson). Copyright © 1977 E. J. Brill. Reprinted by permission of E. J. Brill, Leiden and HarperCollins Publishers Inc., New York.

Breitenbush Books: Excerpt from WEN FU: THE ART OF WRITING by Lu Chi, trans. from the Chinese by Sam Hamill. Copyright © Sam Hamill.

Jonathan Cape Ltd: Excerpt from THE HEART OF THE WORLD by Alan Ereira. Copyright © 1990 Alan Ereira. Reprinted by kind permission of Random House, UK Ltd.

Carcanet Press Ltd: Excerpt from THE GOLDEN ASS by Robert Graves. Copyright © 1950 Robert Graves. Reprinted by permission of Carcanet Press Ltd, Manchester, on behalf of the Trustees of the Robert Graves Copyright Trust.

Editions du Cerf, Paris: Poem to Hathor from HYMNES ET PRIERES DE L'EGYPTE ANCIENNE by A. Barucq and F. Dumas. Copyright © 1980 A. Barucq and F. Dumas.

Element Books: Excerpt from TAO TE CHING by Man-Ho Kwok, Martin Palmer, and Jay Ramsay. Copyright © 1993 Man-Ho Kwok, Martin Palmer, and Jay Ramsay. Reprinted by permission of Element Books, Shaftesbury, Dorset, and Rockport, Mass.

HarperCollins Publishers: Excerpt from INANNA, QUEEN OF HEAVEN AND EARTH by D. Wolkstein and S. M. Kramer. Copyright © 1983 D. Wolkstein and S. M. Kramer. Reprinted by permission of Diane Wolkstein.

HarperCollins Publishers Ltd: Excerpt from KUAN YIN by Martin Palmer, Jay Ramsay, and Man-Ho Kwok, 1995. Copyright © 1995 Martin Palmer, Jay Ramsay, and Man-Ho Kwok. Reprinted by permission of HarperCollins Publishers Ltd, London.

HarperCollins Publishers: Except from WOMEN IN PRAISE OF THE SACRED by Jane Hirshfield. Copyright © 1994 Jane Hirshfield. Reprinted by permission of Jane Hirshfield and HarperCollins Publishers, Inc., New York.

Alfred A. Knopf, Inc.: Excerpts from TAO TE CHING by Lao Tzu, trans. from the Chinese by Gia Fu-Feng and Jane English. Reprinted by permission of Alfred A. Knopf, Inc., New York.

Shambhala Publications Inc.: Excerpts from THE BOOK OF THE HEART by Loy Ching-Yuen, trans. from the Chinese by Trevor Carolan and Bella Chen. Copyright © 1988, 1990 Trevor Carolan and Bella Chen. Excerpts from AWAKENING TO THE TAO by Liu I-Ming, trans. from the Chinese by Thomas Cleary. Copyright © 1988 Thomas Cleary. Reprinted by permission of Shambhala Publications Inc., Boston, Mass.

Thames and Hudson Ltd: Excerpt from EGYPTIAN MYSTERIES by Lucy Lamy. Copyright © Lucy Lamy 1981. Reprinted by permission of Thames and Hudson, London.

University of California Press: Excerpt from THE POETRY OF SUMER: CREATION, GLORIFICATION, ADORATION by Samuel Kramer. Copyright © 1979 The Regents of the University of California. Reprinted by permission of University of California Press, Berkeley, CA.

University of Chicago Press: Excerpt from KINGSHIP AND THE GODS by Henri Frankfort. Copyright © 1976 Henri Frankfort. Reprinted by permission of University of Chicago Press, Chicago, Ill.

Wildwood House Ltd: Excerpts from CREATIVITY AND TAOISM by Chang Chung-yuan. Copyright © 1963 Chang Chung-yuan (now out of print). Excerpts from TAO TE CHING by Lao Tzu, trans. from the Chinese by Gia Fu-Feng and Jane English. Copyright © 1972 Gia Fu-Feng and Jane English. Reprinted by permission of Wildwood House Ltd, Aldershot, Hampshire.

University Press of New England: Excerpts from HYMNS TO ISIS IN HER TEMPLE AT PHILAE, trans. by Louis V. Zabkar. Copyright © 1988 Louis V. Zabkar. Reprinted by permission of University Press of New England, Hanover, New Hampshire.

The passages from The Wisdom of Jesus Ben Sirach and The Wisdom of Solomon follow the King James version and are arranged as in THE BIBLE DESIGNED TO BE READ AS LITERATURE, edited by Ernest Sutherland Bates, published by William Heinemann Ltd, London (no date).

The excerpts from Enheduanna's poems "The Exaltation of Inanna," "Inanna and Ebeh," and "Lady of Largest Heart" are from an unpublished manuscript called INANNA, LADY OF LARGEST HEART. The rendition of the poems is by B. De Shong Meador, with translations and assistance by D. Foxvog. The excerpt from the poem "Lady of Largest Heart" has been published in UNCURSING THE DARK by B. De Shong Meador, Chiron Publications, Wilmette, Ill.

The poem translated by Stephen Langdon comes from SUMERIAN AND BABYLONIAN PSALMS by Stephen Langdon, published by Librairie Paul Geuthner, Paris, 1909.

The hymn to Ishtar is from L. W. King, THE SEVEN TABLETS OF CREATION, London, 1902.

We would like to thank Dr. Dusan Pajin for his thesis on Kuan Yin and Sukie Colegrave for her book THE SPIRIT OF THE VALLEY (Virago, 1979)